I0640067

Kegan Paul

Songs of Coming Day

Kegan Paul

Songs of Coming Day

ISBN/EAN: 9783744768054

Printed in Europe, USA, Canada, Australia, Japan

Cover: Foto ©Andreas Hilbeck / pixelio.de

More available books at **www.hansebooks.com**

SONGS OF COMING DAY

a

SONGS OF COMING DAY

LONDON

KEGAN PAUL, TRENCH & CO., 1, PATERNOSTER SQUARE

1885

PREFACE.

———◦◦◦———

IN offering this little volume to the public I beg to say that I do so because it seems to me that whatever we have—however slight the gift—should be used freely for others, to whom it may prove of some good or enjoyment. Therefore, though somewhat late in life, I give these poems—several of which were written years ago—willingly; yet in one sense unwillingly, having no desire to be known as poet or poetaster, not being a youth who sets his foot on the first rung of the ladder of fame, ambitious to climb higher.

Therefore, good public, leave me in obscurity if you will; only if there be any good in this work, take what honey you may chance to find, make it your own, and leave the rest to perish unknown. As for criticism, I seldom read reviews; but sound honest criticism should always be as welcome as it is rare.

Your servant,

THE AUTHOR.

CONTENTS.

	PAGE
OFFERINGS	1
GREEKS	3
THE LEGEND OF ST. BASLE	5
"I HAVE SAID YE ARE GOD'S"	8
DEATH OR LIFE ...	9
A TALE OF REAL LIFE	10
"'TIS WE MUSICIANS KNOW"...	13
OPINIONS	16
UNITY AND PEACE	17
THE WAVE AND THE ROCK ...	18
ONE-SIDED	23
CO-OPERATION	32
DEATH AND LIFE	34
HERAKLES	36
DESIRE	40
LIFE WORTH LIVING	42
A LOVER'S LAMENT FOR HIS SWEETHEART	44
TO-DAY AND TO-MORROW ...	52
THE IMPROVISATRICE	56
BROTHERHOOD	62

	PAGE
THE UNKNOWN GOD	63
THE SIBYL	65
THE DAWNING LIGHT	98
FAILURE	100
THE DEAD LION	102
THE SECRET OF HUMANITY	105
ST. BRIAVAL'S BELLS	109
OUT OF ETERNITY	116
DEATH	118
IF LOVE COULD REIGN	119
TO MAZZINI	123
SONNET	126
SONNET	127
SONNET	128
SONNET ... ...:	129
WRECKS	130
NIGHT COMETH	133
SUNRISE	135
SUDDEN DEATH	136
A WALL OF GLASS	138
FREEDOM	140
TO THE NATIONS !—ANARCHY	142
SACRIFICE	144
MOTHER EARTH	147
ALONE	149
FAREWELL	151

Enter an old man leading a flower-girl with a basket of flowers. She sings—

" J'offre ces violettes,

ERRATUM.

Page 55, line 1, *for* "To" *read* "Is."

Rhyme of bygone leisure,
Breath of tranquil pleasure,
As the halcyon's feather
Of fair golden weather.

"Violets, dark violets,
Pale lilies and flowerets,
Roses fresh dew-sprinkled,
Just unclosed and commingled
With carnations fragrant.
It is but a vagrant

B

CONTENTS.

	PAGE
THE UNKNOWN GOD ...	63
THE SIBYL	65
THE DAWNING LIGHT	98
FAILURE	100
THE DEAD LION	102
THE SECRET OF HUMANITY	105
ST. BRIAVAL'S BELLS	109
OUT OF ETERNITY	116
DEATH	118
IF LOVE COULD REIGN	119
TO MAZZINI ...	123
SONNET ...	
SONNET	
SONNET ...	
	136
	138
	140
TO THE NATIONS !—ANARCHY	142
SACRIFICE	144
MOTHER EARTH ...	147
ALONE	149
FAREWELL	151

" J'offre ces violettes,
  Ces lis, et ces fleurettes,
    Et ces roses, icy ;
  Ces vermeillettes roses
  Sont freschement écloses,
    Et ces œillets aussi."

JOACHIM DE BELLAY.

"I BORROW this rhyme
From a far-away time—
Rhyme of bygone leisure,
Breath of tranquil pleasure,
As the halcyon's feather
Of fair golden weather.

"Violets, dark violets,
Pale lilies and flowerets,
Roses fresh dew-sprinkled,
Just unclosed and commingled
With carnations fragrant.
It is but a vagrant

B

"Who offers you flowers;
No pomp and no dowers,
No gift of dull gold,
Yet riches untold !
Nay, in some fair weeds
Lurk the goldenest seeds !

"In hearts of some flowers
May linger true dowers ;
Yet not of my bringing,
No result of *my* singing.
He is gifted with sight
Who knows their sweet light.

"Violets, fresh violets,
Pale lilies and flowerets,
Roses dew-sprinkled,
With rare pinks commingled,—
While I offer you these,
Call them weeds if you please.

"Only fair flowers
From fragrant bowers ;
Only weeds if you will.
Be it yours to fulfil :
Mine but the poor gift,
It is yours to uplift."

GREEKS.

You Greeks of old so calm and clear,
  So fair and free and strong, oh, Greek !
You did not doubt your sunshine here ;
You lived and loved and knew no fear,—

No fear, no doubt ; you found perfection,
  While we search on and vainly seek.
Too much we search, perchance, and question,
Till all we find is imperfection.

As gods ye moved, ye chiselled, wrought—
  Each art complete, divinely Greek ;
But we ! We labouring say, " 'Tis nought !
So far from all we hoped or sought."

Yet for that grand heroic art,
  While ours seems faltering, weak,
We would not forfeit, for our part,
That longing hope which fills the heart.

That passionate hope, almost a rage,
　　Such was not yours, oh, sunny Greek !
Nor yours to yearn, cold tranquil sage,
For the glad ripening of a perfect age ;

Not yours to love the human-kind—
　　Did such love seem too poor and meek ?—
With the strong force of soul and mind :
Love, clear, discerning, true, but never blind.

For all your lovely myths, your songs and lyre,
　　Creative harmony, my Greek,
We would not give that ardent living fire,
Godlike, though human, our long intense desire.

Yet did our Plato dream a noble dream,
　　No mere imaginative freak ;
That free Republic was his goodly theme.
How great, if all unreal it did beseem !

And that keen faith in man's eternal soul,
　　Was it not thine, oh, wisest Greek,—
That faith in which all great men must enroll,
Perfection of our human-kind, the final goal ?

THE LEGEND OF ST. BASLE.

" ANATHEMA, Maranatha ! " words of fate,
  Spoken by his great holiness himself.
Did the poor monk repent ?   Was it too late ?
  But who said he repented ?   Laid on a shelf,
Amongst all vile expurgatories—no weight,
  No worth henceforth, no good for play or pelf,
He died, condemned to suffer pains of hell,
Yet dared with dying breath to say, " 'Tis well."

Now those awaiting Basle's repentant speech
  Have crossed themselves, and shuddering turn
To seek that pious monk who acts as leech.
  " What, truly dead? " they say. " And must he burn
In endless fire—he who was wont to preach
  Of Heaven so well, it were a joy to learn
From one who seemed by Heaven sent to teach ? "
  But that monk sagely turned his head aside,
Saying, " Yet in hell our brother must abide."

Thus talking, no one heard an angel's wing
    Fanning the dead man laid so coldly by.
They know not—while the hope to which they cling
    Is rudely severed, and they dare not sigh—
The angel stoops that poor monk's soul to bring,—
    Where ?   To hell, and there a fitting place descry
Wherein he may suffer, as doomed culprit ought,
The tortures by his contumacy bought.

Arrived—given in ribbed ice to be confined,
    Where shivering naked souls imprisoned pine,
Basle set himself to cheer where all repined :
    He stilled the fiercest, soothed the saddest mind,
Till devils cried, " The sun in hell doth shine ! "
    And angry devil-angels bid him cease ;
    But he, all radiant, wished them joy and peace.

Still he discoursed, so kindly and so well,
    Those evil angels would not work him harm ;
And—thus my legend—good angels almost fell,
    Fluttering too near ; for they, too, felt the charm,
And, listening, said, " Come, let us bide in hell :
    Content and joy are there." Then, seized with alarm,
The angel who had brought him there to abide,
Moved him to where fresh torments joy deride.

But here, amazing to relate, he sang,
    Amidst his pains, such pæons of delight,
That all around him hardly felt a pang,
    And devils in chorus joined, forgetting night.

To the great God of Love and Light they sang,
  Till, far above, the strains of rapture rose,
  And broke even heaven's great and grand repose.

Then an Almighty voice was heard to say,
" Who darkeneth knowledge with false counsel's word ?
Whose folly sent to hellish night a gleam of day?
  'Tis well ; even there must a true soul be heard.
For such there is no hell, no power to slay
  God's life in him, his soul's eternal ray."
They heard, and bowed submissive, none demurred.
  Straightway they bear him home ; he enters there.
  Where ? Nay, his home, like God, is everywhere.

"*I HAVE SAID YE ARE GOD'S.*"

I HAVE said ye are God's, oh, children of light,
What fallen, wandering and lost in the night ?
With visions of splendour, but chiselled in pain,
Wrought in madness or sorrow, not all in vain ;
With brain ardent as fire, yet hands numbed by frost,
Your work may be crippled, it cannot be lost.
Walk bravely, ye artists, work bravely, be free.
Do they say, " Ye are nought "?   Your work is to be,—
To be and to live through a far-seeing age,
Though the people may surge, the people may rage.
What, failure ?   So speak the fond children of earth,
Whose lips no live-coal kindled.   Whence is their birth ?
But ye—ye are God's, and His children of light.
He saith, "Live for ever."   Your work is His might.

DEATH OR LIFE.

WE launched our boat upon an angry sea.
Storm-driving mists hid all the pleasant lea.
Waves, threatening, reared their forms foam-crested :
Fearlessly our bark their fury breasted.
The sea grew leaden-hued. A cloudy pall
From heaven to ocean, even as a wall,
Closed darkly in our course. "See there," said one,
"Thus death shuts off man's race half run, half won,—
Cuts it athwart, and flings him as a jest
For men and gods to laugh at his poor best."
A rift ! The pall was parted, rent asunder ;
Beyond, all light, fair fields, a glowing wonder.
Was it death or life that opened to our eyes ?
Say rather, life in death, man's longed-for prize.

A TALE OF REAL LIFE.

HE were a poacher an' a smuggler too.
I loved un.   To last day my love must rue,
For Justice still will him and me pursue,
Though it starve me and my children, not a few.

He were a handsome fellow till the brand
Had scored his brow and red blood stained his hand :
As good as you, my noble sir, so grand,
When he first snared a hare on the parson's land.

It were a cruel winter, stormy cold,
No work for him.   An' he were not that bold
Nor mean to ask for help ; rather we sold
Our little traps for bread.   With grief untold

We heard the babies cry for bread in vain ;
And then my man rose mighty in his pain.
Sure once it seemed he'd do nought ill for gain—
How could I guess they'd turn him to a Cain ?

It were but stormy, yet when morning shone
He left me sleepin', for he heard me moan.
I woke to hear him stride out with a groan.
That night he came not; I were all alone.

He'd snared a hare, so Parson had him took,
Just as he'd nigh got safe across the brook
Which parts Parson's land from Shepherd's Clover-nook ;
And when they told me, I turned cold and shook,

For well I knew it wouldn't all end there.
When he came back to find us mostly bare,
He told me how, in prison, mad with care,
He swore an oath, and only thought it fair,—

While preaching men still talk so fast and loud
Of Christ and Christ's work, yet plainly show the crowd,
The piteous crowd in bitter troubles bowed,
That Christ, indeed, from out His long-worn shroud,

Does not arise, for no Christ can be found,—
A fair oath, so he said, he swore by God's wound,
No more he'd work for man or till his ground,
But fight for's own, as he were sorely bound.

Then adown my cheeks tears poured like rain ;
I pleaded long, but all—yes, all in vain.
He kissed me hard, but answered none again.
He went.—One sore sad night returned to me a Cain.

Now, none knowed but me, they so little knew
Or guessed.   An' yet my fears all doubled grew,
Lest blood should cry from him my master slew.
Why feared I, then, for none could prove it true ?

But now, as I see him lean again' that post,
My stars ! but one 'ud think he'd seen a ghost !
How he peers over t'shoulder ! I'd a'most
He'd seen one and be done.   I see a host,

A host of ghosts—my fears.   I get no rest.
And yet—I love him still, though he may be a pest
He drinks ; he has a cruel mouth at best ;
Not handsome now, he's but an ugly guest ;—

What matters all ?   I love him true an' fast.
If Church an' Law be hard (they forget no past),
I care no whit for all the stones they cast :
I clasp him tight, and hold on to the last.

Maybe before he dies his sin he'll see ;
But now, when they tell him Heaven's wrath to flee,
He don't care a jot—not he, he says, not he.
Why should us care ?   There's allays wrath enough for we.

Seems that if Christ's, God's love—how parsons prate
An' never make it clear till all's too late—
If God's love, as they say, be strong and great,
He'll hold us fast through all, me an' my mate.

"'TIS WE MUSICIANS KNOW."

Sea breezes, pine breezes, mingled together ;
Free breezes, moorland breeze over the heather ;
Bright amber water murmuring and flowing ;
Red browny cattle softlily lowing,
And with, yet apart, distinctly yet airily,
Music, wind-music, commingling fairily.

"Oh, whence is that music I hear, but see nought?"
Then came one who said, "What, buried in thought?"
"Hush ! there's music," he answered. "Silence, and
        listen !"
"Music? What music? Show me fairies that glisten,
In bells of the heather I may see them too ;
But no music I hear. Perchance Doon's merry crew
Is haunting us now with that old rabble rant ;
But their musical powers allow me to doubt.
For few ghosts are, I fancy, finished musicians,
Nor are poets and artists always precisians."
And thus they mocked, and not a sound could hear.
But yet to him those sounds were sweet and clear ;

Familiar, too, they seemed, if somewhat strange.
We travelled on along that purple range
Of Exmoor hills, then came we to a wood
Just as glad Day had doffed her lighter mood
And quiet Evening donned her blue-grey hood.

Where the pines parted, there we stood and gazed
At those long waves of purple; then
He started—there was that music still,
But now with somewhat of triumphant will,
Rousing as if with an electric thrill,
Now clear and ringing, then with softer fall,
Which seemed re-echoed from some rocky wall.

"You hear it now," he said, as they drew nigh.
"Art mad?" they cried. "Ah, Prospero, you sigh!
But we—in no enchanted isle we dwell.
You hear! You only hear your dainty Ariel."

And is it true? Can some indeed thus walk
To sounds of music which in rhythm talk,
Discoursing harmonies to them alone,
While others cannot hear a single tone?
What unheard choir is all around? Oh, soul,
In that grand choir if not thine to enroll
Thyself, be it thine at least to speak
Of what is heard by those who truly seek!
Speak bravely and freely to the strong or weak;
Make of thy very life a perfect song;
Turn all alike to music for the throng

Who have so little ; let them learn from thee
How much all may, but do not, hear or see,
How perfect are those harmonies divine
Which linger near us.   Only while we pine
For clods of earth, deaf, deaf and blind, we live
And know not, have not, thus we cannot give.
But thou, give freely.   If given song and light,
That light melodious should disperse the night.
Unknown !   Doth it to thee sound far and changed,
Its fair notes jarred and all its harmony estranged ?
Fear not, if oftentimes the music, thus unheard,
Seems even lost.   Fear not.   God gives the word—
On the chaotic waters breathes the ghost,
And lo ! there lives and moves a starry host.

OPINIONS.

OPINIONS, changing, come and pass;
Dogmas may tyrannize and amass:
Hear all, bear all, but yield to none.
Believe the pearl of Truth is one.

One God, why call Him by strange names?
One Faith, why blur it with strange claims?
One baptism—water, pain, or fire.
But all we know, all we require,
Is Eternal Goodness, which must reign,
Sooner or later must prevail,
And in man's heart as King remain.
This is the kingdom which we pray
May come.   We yearn, and yet to-day,
Behold, that kingdom is.   But where?
It comes within, and even now is there,—
To him who truly lives and loves,
His own, a kingdom pure and fair.

UNITY AND PEACE.

BRAVE Corcyreans, fiercely fighting men,
Did they then question, with imploring pen,
From what gods or heroes by their prayers
The gift of unity they might obtain—
That gift to be for ever, ever theirs?
And yet it's said they asked but all in vain.
And now, do we not pray and pray for peace?
For unity, peace, we cry, in restless pain.
Will such prayers ever rise, and never cease,
While bleeding tears of war for ever rain?
"What god will give us peace?" we cry again.
They say the God of Love speaks to men peace;
Yet when we echo "Peace!" by war it's slain.
Must we, too, ask, and always plead in vain?

c

THE WAVE AND THE ROCK.

Do you see those shattered stones,
Crumbling like a dead man's bones,
Whitening on the sandy lea,
Deserted by the ebbing sea?

Here once shone a little lake.
Not a wave its stillness brake,
Tranquil in God's light it lay;
Yet around that tranquil bay,
Stormy echoes of the ocean
Told of foreign fierce emotion.
Happy lake, profoundly blest,
Serenely quiet in its rest!
From the outer world no word
With a pang its bosom stirred.

Came a day when, from the headland,
Suddenly a giant hand
Pierced and broke that peaceful life,
Rousing it to painful strife;

For a massive iron stone,
Severed from the parent bone,
Fell amidst the dreaming water
With a deep determined slaughter.
Then that sunny surface cleft,
Of its peaceful calm bereft,
Seemed to shiver into fragments,
Broke in million diamond segments,
While a strong convulsion stirred
Its very depths ; a voice was heard—
" Iron Rock, is this thy will ?
Be it so, thy fate fulfil."
But the bay, once still and dreaming,
All its nature changes, seeming,
And the happy tranquil lake,
Though like a child that, just awake,
Ripples with its startled fears,
Half in laughter, half in tears,
The hardened rock may well beware,
For that lake, so still and fair,
Is now a wave to do and dare.
Day by day that wave is playing,
Round the rock its waters staying,
With the rosy day-dawn gleaming,
Laughing with the noontide's beaming,
Reflex of the late suntide,
Always near it will abide,
Save, at times, its distant moan
Strives to soothe the iron stone.

All in vain; that rippling wave
Cannot soften, cannot save.
All in vain; that fragile spray,
Borrowing brilliance from the day,
Softly clinging to the rock,
Cannot gladden that grey block,
Sullen to all tender teaching,
Deaf to tuneful wild beseeching.
But the compeers of that wave,
All the fair and all the brave,
Call with ringing voices loud—
"Come back, oh, wave! What, queenly proud,
Art thou a vassal chained and bowed?
Come to the glad, the glorious sea,
Where thou mayst be swift, strong, and free;
Come where the golden sands are soft,
Or the white cliffs meet the spray aloft."
Deaf to their calls, the kindly wave
Still circles round, a patient slave,
As glancing up with sunny smile
Stony dulness it would beguile.

Strange to say, in rockiest mood,
Sullen and dark that iron stood,
Till at last the wave became
Stirred by anger or by shame;
Smote with pain, its white crests meeting,
Fiercely surging, madly beating,
O'er that dull untuneful stone,
Till music rung in strongest tone.

Thus it sung : "This cruel stone
Would disturb me when alone—
Quiet, happy, and alone ;
Now it shall at least atone.
Not here my sorrow will I hide,
Nor here for ever will abide :
Since I could not, in my gladness,
Help thee to beguile thy sadness ;
Since I could not be thy joy,
Never will I be thy toy.
But remember, in thy gloom,
Rock, I yet will be thy doom.
Weak, they say, a wave may be ;
Nay, strong, relentless, as the sea.
Though the sea has soft caresses,
She strangles victims in her tresses."

Thus the wave. But wind and tide
In one determined compact bind,
To restore the wavelet to its kind.
Blindly and madly still the wave
Clings to the rock it yet would save.
Desperate its struggles, but at last
Both wind and tide have seized it fast ;
The rock is stranded on the shore,
The wave is at its feet no more.

Some say the wave once broke away,
And, like a tiger on its prey,

Sprang on the rock and tore it there,
Laying its deep recesses bare.
And then it sought the sunny sea,
And laughed away a life of glee.
Some say the rock remained alone,
Till, sudden, snapped its heart of stone,
And lo ! that wave had worn away
A rift that let in light of day ;
Then prone amidst the sands it lay,
No wave to chaunt its funeral knell.
Yet others tell, though but the few,
That wave still lingered kind and true ;
Spent, sad, and tired, its parting sigh
Moaned as it rippled slowly by ;
And when the rock fell crumbling here,
Its dying murmur sounded near.

ONE-SIDED.

THE LAMENTATION OF A MAD SOMETIME DEMOCRAT WHO, HAVING
GIVEN HIS ALL TO THE CAUSE, HAS LOST HIS LEADER, HIS
LOVE, AND HIS FAITH.

SHALL I tell you, you who spend
Your pity on some world to mend,
World of creatures little better
Than the beasts you feed and tether;
Shall I tell you what is grief,
What is loss without relief?

A grand soul dead !
My comrade and friend, with life's vigour rife,
What a world of lead !
This world only yesterday teeming with life,
Heavy as clay and grim as dull night;
Heavy mountain and breezeless tree,
Heavy the earth and the dull grey sea ;
Heavy even the autumn-day's light ;
And where then should all life flee,
But afar with thee ?

Ay, fled away.
All lost to me his strong full life and power.
Seems but yesterday,
Was he not in his manhood's perfect flower?
We climbed the Alps together.   His mirth
Made toil and danger seem a jest.
Godlike his strength; what godlike zest!
Surely no son of our dull earth;
Yet to-day that earth must rest
Upon his breast.

What dismal weather!
Comrade, when in that course, a goodish stride—
You weighed no feather—
You took the big brook, you would deride
As a poor streamlet, I did not dream
That puny men with their captious blight
Would kill strength and brain in petty fight,
Crush out such light like a farthing gleam,
And send it all to utter night.
Farewell, my light.

Yes, you had brain,
Brain that would suffice a score of common men.
Not all in vain
You spoke; and then you wielded such a pen.
Oh, king among a race of dwarfs and fools,
Who never crowned you for their king,
Who never made your joy-bells ring,

Forgive them, for they were but tools.
Among them all your wealth you'd fling
    With true gold's ring.

        Dead, dead my king!
Too late their fulsome praises sound ;
        Too late bells ring,
Only to toll in muffled round,
While I alone to covert side
        Through fog must ride.

And yet you marvel that I hold
That dull and half-souled crowd of men,
But little worth beside the cold
Remains of this my friend, who, when
He lived, was worth them all, if sold ;
Yet that's not all, for yet another
I have to mourn besides that brother.

Thy name to breathe upon the air,
My sweet, I hardly dare aloud,
Thou liest there so still and fair.
        My queenly fair,
Thou art so quiet in thy shroud,
So tranquil in thy beauty rare,
While hurries by the noisy crowd,
        So loud, so loud.

Thy loving woman's heart is still,
Thy manly brain can work no more ;
No more thou spendst thyself at will
    Our lives to fill.
A lovely vision !   Close the door ;
Shut it close, for a deadly chill
Is on the world, and my heart's core
    Will leave no more.

Men did not recognize thy crown ;
That little crown of golden hair
Was all they knew of thy renown,
    Thy priceless crown.
Was it unfair that in my care
I kept thee from the careless town,
So ill could I thy sweetness spare,
    Unfair, unfair ?

Was it unfair, thus kept apart
From all the thoughtless talking throng ?
If so, I doubly feel the smart
    That wrings my heart.
Was that unfair?   I loved so long,
I hid my talent in my heart.
For me alone she sang her song.
    Was I so wrong ?

But was I wrong?   Without a peer,
Her form, her face, her simple grace,

Her wit, her wisdom. Did I fear
      For one so dear?
None like to her.   Her perfect face—
How could they know?   Yet it was clear
That even our sordid, stupid race
      Would give her place.

Aye, they gave her place.   Was that my dread,
That the world my pearl should freely use,
And set this pearl in brass or lead,
      Like some fool's head ;
Or in their sour champagne infuse
My pearl of price, which they might shed
For fools to drink, or waste and lose,
      And then abuse?

It made me mad to think that child,
Thus used, might have been lost or sold ;
And yet it almost drives me wild.
      This gold three-piled,
This perfect treasure of pure gold,
Such soul, such brain, heart undefiled,
Was chipped and used, aye, used tenfold,
      Though gold, pure gold.

In common household petty care,
We used her gems, as if indeed
They were but earthen common ware,
      Though gems so rare.

We did not mean it, for her speed,
Her ease in work, proved but a snare,
Rendering us thoughtless to take heed
          Of gems indeed.

Could the world do worse, or rather more,
We tried it, and it seemed that where
She smiled, there opened each closed door,
          Though sealed before.
True, for that world she could not care.
For prey the cagèd beasts may roar,
But Wisdom will not enter there.
          How could she care?

But what use in lamentation's woe?
A democrat once, I cried aloud
At kings and queens, and crowds that grow
          So low, so low.
But now amongst that brutal crowd,
I bow my head as low, as low,
While in my grief I speak aloud
          To that low crowd.

Ye brutes, that eat and drink and die,
What are ye to my king and queen?
You cry for help, for freedom try—
          False cry, false cry!—
And take no heed of such half-seen
Angelic lost ones, once so nigh
Lost, but worth crowds of false and mean,—
          False, false, I ween.

Talk not of race, of worms that crawl ;
Great natures, noble hearts and brains,
You waste, you sacrifice them all
  At blockheads' call,
To make helpless Abels and murderous Cains,
Who howl, "Let evil curses fall
On our lauded foes who hold our gains."
  Naught for our pains.

Cains, but never one quiet Seth.
Full of windy talk they mop and mow,
Puffed-up, paltry children of Heth.
  Come, Death, sweet Death.
In the Commons I curse that vapid flow
Of rotten discourse, it chokes my breath.
They make me long, while their tares they sow,
  Kind Death to know.

But great ones amid their noble toil
Die crushed out by their petty worry,
Hustled, destroyed by their sad moil,
  Turmoil, turmoil.
The crowds go by in hideous hurry—
Besotted crowds ; this earth they soil,
They kill all brain with heat and flurry,
  And senseless worry.

They would raze the green sequestered wood,
They would spoil the park and drain the tarn,

To give the dwindled blockheads food—
　　Food, poor and crude.
You wonder that I rave and mourn,
You take exception to my mood,
I, most of all men that are born,
　　Forlorn, forlorn.

I tell you, who would reform the race,
Teach men to live, not run to seed,
Teach them their energies to brace,
　　Poor race, poor race !
But as greater ones you would not heed,
I do not ask for breathing space,
In truth, I have but little need—
　　So little need.

What use to bid these madmen cease,
Since she who pitied each poor devil
Was, though she loved sweet Nature's peace—
　　She craved for peace—
Too freely spent to save from peril
Some sheep with torn and ragged fleece,
She loving joy's light gladsome revel,
　　Free Nature's revel.

And he who shared strong Nature's life,
Left all to stew in that "Our Village,"
Wasting and waning in its strife—
　　War to the knife—

The commonwealth. Some phrase of tillage,
Of sowing, reaping, to hide the knife,
For they always end in strife and pillage,
    War's mad tillage.

I am almost glad they are both dead ;
I could not bear to see them spent,
Like pelicans their life-blood shed,
    And their hearts shred.
Would I thus see them torn and rent?
Rather with them would I lay my head,
And leave the world its argument
    On life-blood spent.

CO-OPERATION.

RAISE the cry, be this your song,
Part all lands to give the throng—
The throng of starving ones who wait
All day long outside the gate.
Good; but, giving each one his share,
Think you enough with none to spare,
Barely enough, will yet be there?
I tell you, nay, for such is man,
Some grasping and gaining all they can,
Make gold where others starve and long;
The cure must come for all this wrong.
But it is this, now heed it well,
We cannot long the truth expel.

Servants of all, not for their pleasure
Have some received in fullest measure.
Then faithfully expend your treasure,
All you who have, or land, or gold,
And learn you must this service hold.

Co-operate with all around ;
Let every one that tills the ground
Reap a fair share of fruit and seed ;
Let every workman have his meed,
His share in factory, mart, and bale.
Then, only then, we shall not fail,
As brothers live.   If this we learn,
We cease to crave and lust and burn.

No law can property divide,
With use and safety to abide.
All law greed always will deride,
Save the law of love, which makes men live
As brethren, and free justice give.

DEATH AND LIFE.

DEEP night was on my soul.   Sorrow and Death,
  Like two sad sentinels, held me in thrall.
It seemed as though I could not draw a breath,
  So prisoned was I by their dungeon wall;
So stifled in their cruel icy grasp
  I could not speak, yet heard the seabirds call,
  And ringing rocks below the quarry fall.

For it was day ; the low sky seemed to wrap
  As it were, in one grey pall of cloud,
Hills, fair fields, red rocks, and even waves to hap,
  Thus their loveliness and valour to enshroud.
Winds moaned, and my sad over-burdened heart,
  Though sternly bowed, submissive to hard fate,
With inward moan, still seemed of them a part.
  Then on the air there rose what well might grate
On weary sense, the rhythm of a chime
As if defying death, and age, and time.

A chime of bells, with joy and gladness rife.
I raised my head.   Behold, all light and life.
Clouds parted, glowing light touched sea and land,
While rocks and sea a rainbow arch had spanned.
Strong from my bitter anguish then I rose,
And knew what airy phantoms were my foes.
Sorrow no more, I said, for death is life,
Death is not, though he seems to bring wild strife
Of anguished loss.   'Tis but another name for life.
We dullards cannot see through tear-beclouded eyes.
True friend, dear love and life, that comes in this disguise.

HERAKLES.

DID the gods give the strong hero, in his early youth,
   his choice—
Hard toil, or some voluptuous life of ease? When he
   found voice
To speak, did he faltering pause? Did he shudder in
   amaze,
As with prophetic wistful eyes he gazed along life's
   troubled ways?
Nay; though only a demigod, and keen to suffer mortal
   woes,
He did not shrink, but chose, and forthwith armed him
   to encounter foes.
He paused not. Henceforth, far or near, or low or high,
   that work he sought.
Hero or man, such work is never vain, it cannot end in
   nought.
With godlike eyes, clear in their eagle might, discerning,
   seeing,
He nerved his strong sinews and his frame to the stern
   task of being;

To his firm purpose he allowed no stint, thus strengthened
　　to endure.
Had he, then, early learned the costly price of pleasure's
　　sweet allure ?
Yet that hero, who Augean stables could purify and purge,
Who hydra-headed evil could destroy, knew hydra-
　　passions' scourge.
Aye, truly ; yet he laboured on. " Ye gods, befriend him ;
　　grant him grace ! "
Thus surely men and women prayed, that he might win
　　his race.
He won, but through what throes of passion, passion
　　strong and half subdued !
The Nessus shirt of vengeance, by his own poison deep
　　imbued,
Awaited him ; dear gift of burning love, of jealous fear
　　and wile,
For which no cure was to be found, but his last couch
　　the fiery pile.
Thus through long labours and fierce pangs, Herakles
　　learned that, to the great,
Work and submit are words of law. He bent submissive
　　to his fate,
Stern demigod, by mortal weakness trapped, by mortal
　　weakness slain.
Didst ever weary of thy tasks ? Did ever mortal craven
　　doubt
Subdue the arm that nobly slaved, and slew the savage
　　rabble rout?

Did that strong form of earthly flesh quench thy clear
    spirit's finer force ?
Did that glad living, full and free, leave room for doubt,
    or fear of loss ?
Brave hero, the cankering ill within, not mortal ill
    without ;
Thy own fierce hates, and fiercer loves, not Dejanira's
    fond desire,
Not foolish tasks from fickle gods, not angry Juno's
    fretful ire,
Were spells to work thee ill, and burn thy flesh with
    festering fire.
Thine, only thine, the fatal snares that trapped and
    finally destroyed.
But yet, what fresh life waits to greet thee ?   Work and
    love both unalloyed !
Thus, then, the hero wakes in him, to fuller life and
    strong content,
As, making ready to depart, knowing at last how that fair
    tent
Of human flesh was but a cumbrous coil that weighed
    his godlike soul,
Serenely now, in patience, waits Jove's car to bear him to
    his goal.   .
He, resting on the pile, shrinks not from fires that thus
    his past anneal.
Thence rose the demigod with all his greatness freshly
    to reveal.

Did he regret those labours past, or curse the cause of
  his death-throes ?
Rather, rejoicing in that past, he knew the wisdom of his
  woes.
" Ye gods," man cries, "give me all good and mirthful
  many-coloured days !
Give the sweet wine of life !"   Man quaffs the draught,
  and bitterly he pays.
But some—" Give us not merely rest, nor pleasure's
  lusty careless joy,
But the strong tide of fullest life and toil, even with
  pain's alloy ;
Give us that full and fervent tide, oh, give us vivid
  labour's life,
Fain would we plunge therein, and face alike its danger
  and its strife.
Hear us, great God of Love and Light !   Grant us our
  wish, and give us might,
The might to work.   Goodness divine, grant us all this,
  with time and light—
Time, light, to choose and to discern the toilsome but the
  upward way ;
Some calm of night, brief thoughtful rest, yet the great
  light of perfect day."

DESIRE.

In the inn parlour we sheltered from a storm of rain
    and hail,
While, in the gloaming, men told a tale which made some
    quail and pale,—
How, on a moonlight night, they seemed to see strange
    phantoms passing nigh :
One, passion torn, fever spent, wasted and weary, hurry-
    ing by,
Following a phantom fair, far in advance, yet still in
    view,
Who led him on and on, while close on his heels there
    trod a crew—
A ghastly rout. She laughing, they shout louder, follow-
    ing fast,
With gibes and laughter. Then they hear a clear voice
    rise above the blast—
" Pitiful one, so far astray, thus hunted by a ghastly
    crew,
Let fond Desire waste your soul, let but her phantoms
    still pursue,

Famished Desire's favours false will lure you to your very grave,

There tread you fiercely down, while curses the earth above you pave."

But True Desire, thus revealed, as she stood before him half removed,

Yet in his path, then softly said, "Has life indeed enough been proved?

Do you know me now? Not poor Desire, for human wealth and pelf;

But rich Desire, all human love, your second but your greater self.

Alas! few know me thus, for the many still in anguish cry,

'We long, we waste our lives for thee; with passionate grief we sigh.'

They know me not. With feverish thirst, their gasping wailing cry

Asks the Circean cup which fails the thirst, till of that thirst they die."

They said her face, as well as voice, then with a winning smile would say—

"Come now, for thou must work with me; love, live, and strive with me to-day.

Then, when thy very life is mine, when thou canst lay it on my shrine,

Conqueror arise, I am thine own; my treasure is for ever thine."

LIFE WORTH LIVING.

SAGE, do you tell me life is but a page of grey?
Or if the dense clouds sudden seem to part to-day,
And sunshine glimmers fair along our pleasant way,

You say they will return in storms to-morrow—
If joy is near prepare for floods of sorrow?
And thus, my sage, you will not let us borrow.

One ray of gladness from out your thunder-cloud.
Yet even the thunder does not seem too proud
To allow a gleam of sun to adorn its shroud.

But you know nought of those joys, I will be sworn,
To rise and elastic-footed meet the dawn
On the high Alp, where feet of chamois and its fawn,

Or ptarmigan, alone have touched the virgin snow.
How, then, can you know the joyful rush and flow
Of glacier streams, where only snow-flowers grow?

Nor can you know, philosophic owls that hoot,
How good it is to leap the crevasse with light foot,
And speed along the glistening icy shoot.

Then that delicious plunge, after an Alpine march,
In a clear, cool torrent, where beneath the larch
A quiet pool among the rocks rewards your search.

Do you ever breast strong waves of ocean's tide,
While your vigorous arms those healthful waves divide,
And as you crest each wave, you fling "black care"
    aside?

Or has your taut boat, with her heavy spray-wet sheet
And flooded gunwale—your own sea-courser fleet—
Cut a clear way among the waves she seems to beat?

Have you ever known your horse's strong delight
Vibrating through your limbs with sinewy might,
His will and action one with yours, and yours by right,

As he scents the autumn breeze? "Hark away!" the
    hounds!
Sweet that musical bay which through the air resounds!
How goodly is this stride, these free elastic bounds!

What is life worth? Worth living, having, being;
Life that sets pulses throbbing, powers freeing.
Do ears, then, tire of hearing, or eyes of seeing?

Dyspeptic pessimist, in spite of all you write,
Life is a rapture, and a full and free delight.
So strong and free in lusty vigour, manhood's might.

A LOVER'S LAMENT FOR HIS SWEETHEART.

WHAT was my love? you ask me;
Was she like other women?
She was my love, my sweetheart;
She was not like any woman,
But type of what women should be.
Can I say if dusky or fair,
Grave or gay, or witty or wise,
Lovely and little, queenly and tall,
For was she not all of these?
Only never foolish or dull.
For when in the shade she rested,
Her eyes were dark and dreamy,
And her hair like dusky night;
But when in the sunlight standing,
Ah me! she was sunshine itself.
In her hair the sunlight lingered
Lovingly, fondly, caressing,
Till it shimmered and gleamed with gold—

Gold mingled with darkest brown.
But her eyes? I could not tell you
What colour those eyes might be,
For the lovely, wistful meaning,
The glamour, the wonderful light,
Which made those eyes so peerless.
Not violet, blue, with lashes dark.
Simply, that I cannot describe
The soul with its ardent longing,
The mind with its deepest meaning,
The heart with its passionate power.
Grey eyes? In sorrow dark as midnight,
But in anger alight with fire.
In thought deep wells reflecting
Some far-off star-like world;
Then brimming with joy and laughter,
Like flowers in sunny May.
Why talk of her red, red lips,
Or the hue like June's wild roses,
Which blushed in her winsome face,
Though indeed I have seen her as white
As some snowy Alp at twilight.
No; it was not any of these,
Mere shows of colour and form,
That held me enchained, her thrall,
And bound me to her for ever.
But that happy smile God gave her,
That soul shining through the temple,
Speaking in every gesture.

No doubt she was tall and queenly,
As some say women should be,
And yet many called her little.
Little! Oh me! my little one—
Was it love, or were they deceived
By her light and lithesome stature
So perfectly framed and fashioned?
And all her movements elastic
Were full of health and delight;
Yet those active pliant limbs,
With their subtle curves and graces,
Often gave you a notion—
Was it of something of languor,
.   Or was it of perfect repose?

What said the world to my goddess—
'   The shrewd and pitiless world?
It only said, "How clever,
Beautiful, graceful, she is!
We must have her to grace our feasts."
And yet it would have stabbed her
With petty poignards of malice!
But her brave soul wore an armour—
God's truth, pure love, that armour.
Clever! They did not know her,
Those clever, old-world children.
How indeed could they truly know
Her great and lovely soul?
She gave them freely and nobly,

Fair gifts of mirth and gladness,
Free gifts, though rarely, of thought.
Then they only laughed and wondered.
But now I am almost glad,
So little they understood her,
That she never could be theirs,
But only mine, mine only ;
For I, and I only, knew her.
I knew that behind that brow,
Formed like some old Greek model—
Pallas, Athenæ, nothing less—
There lurked the brain of a man.
Of a man, no common man,
But rather another Plato.
And yet to hear her talking
With the herd of men and women !

It was not indeed that she stooped,
But rather in that she felt
With them in their joys and sorrows,
And spoke as if to her fellows.
But what, then ? did you imagine
That in stilted pride she moved,
Like the goddess that she was,
Above all the poor crowd below,
In a solemn dignity sheathed ?
But you should have heard her laugh—
Like a rippling wave its music.
Oh, to see her in the garden

On an early summer's morning,
As she kissed the half-closed buds,
And let the golden laburnums
Sweep over her sunny face,
Then shook the dew from her hair,
And talked and laughed with the birds,
Like a happy innocent child.
Yet in the haunts of sorrow,
Sorrow and sickness and care,
She was patient, loving, and tender,
As if God had sent her to heal.
And her voice had a low vibration,
As if touching some minor chords,
Or like sounds of Eolian harps.
Yet have I seen her a wilding;
Yes, wild with the joy of living.
She could hunt as well as a man;
Nay, rather like a new Diana.
She and her horse were as one,
Full of pliable ease and freedom,
Which made movement lovely to see.
She would dance with the joyful grace,
Not of a woman care-laden,
But rather some happy child.
Sweet child, and woman, and goddess.
Yes, indeed, I am almost glad
That only I understood her.
And can I truly say
That any one really knew her?

That beautiful, manly soul,
With the great brave heart of a man,
Which beat in a woman's breast.

It is true she paid the forfeit
Of all such grander. spirits—
She was somewhat alone in the world.
Aye, alone, and very lonely.
And yet, do you think that she wasted
Herself in a feeble self pity?
When she sat quite alone, apart,
Was there almost an air of sadness,
Homeless longing and sadness,
Which clouded her sweet, bright face,
While her eyes looked far and wistful?
And yet anon there would come
A sudden light in that face,
As if she saw plainly, and knew
That God had not left her alone,—
Not really alone and homeless.
Did I say that she had no faults?
Faults, indeed, my beautiful one!
How wild and wayward she could be!
But I loved her all the better.

And now what more do you ask?
Can I not now forget her?
Forget! When I cease to see and hear,
Then, perchance, I may learn to forget.

E

But now, in the wave's low murmur,
On a quiet autumn night,
I hear her sweet voice singing.
Or when that wave comes dancing
Over the pebbles some summer day,
Again I hear her laughter,
Her rippling, joyous laughter.
But when those waves are curving
Their white crests in the breeze,
I see her slight form swaying
As she stands erect at the helm
Of some light bark she is steering.
For thus have I often seen her.
And when I scent the lilac,
Or fragrant golden laburnum,
Again I seem to perceive
That the breeze has blown back her hair,
And shaken out its perfume.
Or when in the early morning,
I find the June wild roses
Unfaded, blushing, and sparkling
With dewdrops, diamonded over,
I see her, and then I greet her,
Among the rosy larch tassels,
Or among the fresh-grown green
Of the young and sheathed corn.
Or again in early autumn,
Against a gold sheaf leaning,
With hands full of corn and poppies.

Or afar on some mountain brow,
Firm feet on a snowy ridge.
Oh, everywhere.   There she is,
I see her.   But, oh ! I hear her
In the song of the dusky bird ;
In the wind's low voice at evening,
Among elms or pines, I hear her ;
In the quick and joyous call
Of the little blue bird, I hear her ;
And in the silvery notes
Of the river among the reeds.
In the rain I hear the patter
Of her arched and slender feet.
But the sunshine and rain alike
Recall her fair April face,
Till my heart can only ache.
Nature says—" Never forget her,
She was part of me.   Here I am,
And you never shall forget her."
But I also think she was God's.
Perhaps God—God only—knew her.
Shall I grieve that He loved her well?
And when our rude touch hurt her,
Sent Death with white arms wreathing,
Cool, kindly enclasping arms,
And folded His child to rest.

TO-DAY AND TO-MORROW.

WE were living a gay yet turbid life,
Amidst much of folly and more of strife.
They gave me a theme, and this was the text
Which to my poem was duly annext.

" To-morrow, and to-morrow, and to-morrow,
Creeps in this petty pace from day to day ;
   *   *   *   *   *
And all our yesterdays have lighted fools
The way to dusty death.   Out, out, brief candle."

This my text, and thus I preach—
Go, you have no need to teach.
Brief and hurried be my day ;
Stay me not, then, in my way.
Let that day be joy or sorrow,
I reck little of to-morrow.

" Nay," you say, " a mystery
Is clouding your history,

In all your futurity,
Blighting fair maturity."
Oracle of counsel hollow,
Little reck I of to-morrow.

Then you say, "Oh, pause ! oh, pause !
Wait before those opening doors
Of to-morrow.   Let your feet,
Tamed for once, abate their speed."
I tell you, I care not to wait,
Nor to-morrow, what's my fate.

But you still must needs keep looking,
As though my future you were booking
For some distant unknown region.
Despairs and fears you see a legion.
Go, dull prophet, fate's a puzzle.
Silence, then, put on your muzzle.

What ! you start because you think
You see my danger.   On the brink
You see me stand ; see the abyss
Yawn beneath my careless feet.
Close your magic book, this trouble—
Like our life's—a foolish bubble.

Yet a weighty secret certain
Lurks behind yon mighty curtain ;

And if circumstance allowed,
One step and I would pass that shroud.
But as it is I patience borrow,
And so reck little of to-morrow.

Yet I own I'm something tired ;
Somewhat by world's clay bemired.
To be amusèd and amusing ;
Methinks the game is somewhat losing.
On the stage we strut or dangle,
But it isn't worth the candle.

Candle ! Ah, that light translation
Minds me of your first quotation—
" The way to dusty death."—To death ?
You say, this seems to choke your breath.
What cut life short, " out brief candle !"
Will this cure life or only mangle ?

Oh, great master, pardon, pray,
That thus I dare profane your lay ;
There's deep pathos in it, too.
This lit the poor fool on his way
To dusty death.—Put out the light ;
He needs no more, for it is night.

Put out the light—the farce is played.
Come, let us seek night's cooling shade.

To any one at all afraid,
Through the Styx there once to wade?
(Really, friends, you must excuse me ;
If somewhat crazy, don't abuse me.)

In truth my head turns round to think
This is the last.   It makes me shrink.
The last—the past, they make us mad ;
Or is it only—rather sad?
Forgive, I will be, if I can,
" A wiser though a sadder man."

But air is stifling here, and space
Is wanting for our hurried pace.
Give us but air, men say, and room,
We'll ask you not what is our doom.
Rather, give me the thorough present,
I ask not if to-morrow's pleasant.

Good-bye, my friends, join hands and swear
To use the present well, and dare
To face the future, as you may
Blithely and strongly meet to-day.
Then let it be or joy or sorrow,
Bravely will we greet to-morrow.

THE IMPROVISATRICE.

A SKETCH.

THE great hall filled ; the crowds were there,
But where was the Prima Donna—where ?

Draw back that curtain—there within
A young girl stands, nor hears the din
Of careless talk ; her large eyes fill,
Yet her whole posture speaks a will ;
The shapely arms she seems to strain,
With hands clasped tight as if in pain.
She stands unseen, unheard, alone,
By all that crowd unknown, unknown,
And yet determined there to meet,
And with her thoughts that crowd to greet.
The word they give to be her theme
Is life—life, to her no idle dream.
What I then heard but few can know ;
None else were near, nor friend nor foe.

"God give me utterance," she wailed,
And in that cry her voice has failed,
Died as you sometimes hear the gale
Die off in one long passionate wail.
Then, throwing back her queenly head,
" God, I have waited long," she said ;
" Long have I waited, long have tried
To find the utterance thus denied ;
Through other lives have worked my way,
Now shuddering wait the break of day.
Long like a broken harp have lain,
While sweeping all its chords in vain ;
The importunate wind but rouses pain,
Or careless hands for wanton pleasure
Awake some harsh, discordant measure,
Saying, ' You for pleasure were created,
Too slight a toy with wisdom mated.'
So spoke the world, by which thus weighted,
I wandered like a child belated ;
And some reproach this slender frame—
' Too slight for mind's great work.'   Ah, shame !
Were this the case would each strong chord
Thus vibrate to all Nature's word.
God ! only tell me how to utter
All that around me seems to mutter,
Like distant thunder's rolling echoes,
The echoes of all joys and woes ;
Echoes of life's stir and passion,
Echoes of life's weary fashion ;

The empty lustful cry, ' Give more,'
And last sick sigh of man's heart's core.
Whence, then, this throe, and why this pain ?
Must I but live, and live in vain ?
Must I, thrilling with all life,
With its burden and its strife,
With this strong unconquered longing
Of a whole creation thronging
In my heart and in my brain ;
Love of a God, hate of a Cain ;
Tempted Job's long-suffering cursing,
Weary Solomon's vain thirsting,
Unsated youth's living delight,
Its sudden scathing and its blight ;
David's deep, despairing ' Never ! '
And Echo's answer, ' Yet—for ever ' ?

" God, let me breathe ; I choke for air—
For air I wither and despair.
Give me but space—room to declare
All that I know—it is but fair ;
Room, room, there—only let me speak !
O God ! am I too poor and weak ? "
And then she raised her hands on high,
" God ! let me speak but once and die ;
Oh, give me utterance," she sighed,
And with that sigh her voice has died.
She paused, as if she heard a sound,
But her fixed eyes did not glance around ;

She who with strong emotion quivered
Now seemed in some strange way transfigured.

One minute since her smooth white cheek
Had been tinged with red, like some mountain's peak;
One minute since her eager prayer
Rang with keen vibration through the air ;
Her eyes shed a light that struck the sight
Like the fire on some volcano's height.

But now her face was still as night,
And the white light of her soul shone through
That temple of the soul anew.

And thus she moved, how strangely strong,
As she left the room and met the throng ;
No fears, no doubts of her full right
To speak. She stood there calm and bright ;
Like some archangel clothed with light,
Only so childlike in that calm,
Youth's dew on eyelash and youth's balm.
Endowed thus with a wondrous grace,
The full crowd blessed that radiant face.
But she ! She seems to hear a voice,
And hearing only to rejoice,
Such lustre in her shining eyes,
Even her stature seems to rise.
At last she speaks, and then that throng
Hear what is almost like a song,
Set to strange music, deep and strong.

Her words gather, rolling onward,
Softly as in summer upward
Waves rise.   So in harmony arising,
Those mellow tones the crowd surprising,
Give forth new life, as if to rouse
The dead from his last narrow house.
She speaks as some prophet who foreknows
Dark changes near and fearful woes ;
Then bids them fling aside all fear,
Calls them, with notes like clarion clear,
Not to scorn, but boldly danger face,
Meet evil, yielding it no place.
But truly for me it were not meet
Lightly her eloquence to repeat ;
Only, ere her music ceased to ring,
Came words which still to memory cling—
" Oh, men and women, hear again,
In your pleasure or your pain,
Do not let me speak in vain ;
From life there is no rest, relief ;
Life is sweet, some say, and brief ;
I tell you, life is long and endless—
That life so often poor and friendless.
Whence it came from, who can say ?
And yet it marches on to-day,
On in an eternal morrow ;
Out of the ages, perhaps in sorrow,
We have come fresh light to borrow.

Thus man's soul progresses ever;
Who dares to close his course and sever
This from the band who seek perfection,
For all, without stint or selection?
Live, live, and aid man's race to live;
Live bravely, give yourself to give;
Live not for poor imperfect pleasure,
But rich strong life, in fullest measure.
The race of souls *will* live, rejoice,
And you *must* live : there is no choice.
Fear not, for nought can close life—never;
It was, it is, and lasts for ever."
She ceased.   Like a lamp whose light has fled,
Her face became cold, tranquil, dead.
The crowd dispersed.   Some laughed, some cried;
None knew or cared.   That night she died.
Nay, do not grieve; her work was done,
Or rather, with fresh life begun.

BROTHERHOOD.

BROTHERS! those jangling Cains who shriek for a
    commonwealth of prey,
Have long lost sight of aught of brotherhood, but plenty
    pelf and pay.
All who possess they hate; and why? They long to
    have, they long to share.
Yet, trust me, those leeches whose cry is Give, would
    leave their brethren bare.
Their sole idea of commonweal is the false weal of ful-
    some greed;
They ask they know not what, while crushed in their
    grasp lies life's good seed.

O men, who cry for rights of men, begin by resigning
    all your own,
Come down among the ranks of those who in their
    misery lie prone;
Live you their lives, and bravely share rough homes and
    scanty, hard-earned fare;
Then—not till then—go raise your voice, and men may
    heed your prayer.

THE UNKNOWN GOD.

MARCUS AURELIUS, philosopher and friend,
With earnest long intent you sought, and found.
Yet Christians often vainly seek around ;
They scan their books, and call on Heaven to send
The Christ, the God so needed this sad earth to amend.
In vain that unknown God they seek,
Myth-like He hides and will not speak.
Aye, for man makes a God for hate renowned,
Out of his lawless self ; created
In his own image.   Thus belated,
He finds self's idol rudely broken,
And he, still godless, from his dream awoken.

Man, Christian man, in his sententious deeming,
Lost sight of God in all, in Nature's being ;
Lost sight of God in law, and all unseeing,
Of God's harmonious Unity undreaming.
He saw Him not in mountain cloud, or rainbow's sheening,
Nor heard Him in the thunder's might,
Nor knew Him in the starlight night.

From a stern God some madly fleeing,
Found refuge in an idle myth,
In fables fancying kin or kith,
But never God.   Unseen, unknown,
In vain for Him they feebly make their moan.
Yet in one perfect life on earth, it seems
Man might have learned some higher, truer lore,
In lieu of beating wildly at a closèd door,
Thus might have realized all his fondest dreams.
But such a life of love, assorted not with idle schemes,
He lived among the lost and poor ;
Lived, the lame to heal and blind to cure,
With balm for every wound and sore.
He who in mountain desert found relief,
Never shunned the crowds opprest with grief.
But Christians, like Pagans long before,
Set up gods of hate and war—gods to adore.

THE SIBYL.

A FRAGMENT OF ANOTHER POEM.

" Who are these from far away,
Spirits clothed in vapour bright ?
How misty fair their faces gleam,
Gleam like sunlight in the snow.
On their brows rests perfect calm,
Peace, like summer's cloudless dawn,
Breathing of some bygone race,
Beauteous forms of Paradise.
Gods or men ?—immortal are they ?
Giant beauty, giant form,
Mind and soul in mighty mould."

Speaking thus in whispered accents,
Murmuring with a sudden awe,
Stood entranced a weary wanderer.
He had wandered through the day,
Through the live-long summer's day ;
Had been gladdened by the morning,
Had rejoiced in rising dawn.

F

Early fruits and flowers he gathered,
In the purple morning mist,
Rifling them of heaven's nectar,
Freshly dew-distilled nectar.
All around what happy beings,
Like himself in youth and joy,
And with them he chased triumphant—
Chasing shadows to their coverts—
Till with weariness o'ercome,
On the turf he sank to sleep.

Wakening with a strange sensation,
With a sudden sense of grief,
He found all around him changed,
For that blooming wilderness
Was a parched and arid plain.
Here and there some roses lingered,
But they were all fenced with thorns,
Scorched and withering in the sun.
Here a stream once rippling murmured;
Now in stagnant pools it slept,
And a snake was couching there,
Couching at its poisoned source.
In the shade of withered brake,
Still some golden fruit lay scattered,
Flung away by hasty hands;
And hard by lay, crouching fiercely,
Savage beasts to seize their prey.
To and fro this burning desert

Many wandered, feebly moaning,
Or with quick impetuous strides
Hurried on, they knew not whither.
Some, with feverish hurried gaspings,
Sought in sand for buried treasure;
Or they struggled, madly striving
For a bauble nothing worth,
Then beat the air, and shrieking wept.
Some, with burning thirst consumed,
Sought and found polluted streams;
Then they fought to keep possession,
Trampling down the sick and weak.
But as if in bitter mocking
Of victors in that cruel fight,
Those poor waters, hardly won,
Shrank, and dwindling turned to dust.
Springing to his feet, the sleeper
Seized the arm of one he knew.
"Tell me, I conjure thee, tell me,
What is this strange world of woe?
Am I dreaming? Is this true?"
Smiling with a bitter smile,
Said, the other, "Oh, it's true.
You had only seen the morning;
You were blinded by its mists—
Those fair blue and golden mists.
You thus slept a sleep delusive;
All the worse is your awakening.
Now, then, seize on what you may,

Ere this scorching sun has driven
All you care for far away.
Be as merry as you can.
Night is coming ; then, be sure,
Shelter, safety, there is none.
Oh ! you do not fear the night?
Rather, burning sun destroys you,
And this raging thirst betrays you,
And this vexing tide of men—
Captious, fighting crowds of men.
Who's to aid them ?   None, I say.
There's some shade where, densely crowding,
Men and women fight like beasts,
Fighting for an inch of ground.
Better leave them to their fate,
Or they'll rend you as you stand."
" Who are those sad-faced ones, marching
In single file across the plain ? "
" Crazy seekers, are those beings,
For a fancied far-famed fountain.
There are fools who say it lives ;
But so many paths, and devious,
Lead you on the way thereto,
That only piteous madmen seek it,
To find their deathbed and their graves.
For myself, it is enough
Here to struggle for my own.
Still you talk of aiding men !
That were worse than madmen's craze.

See, I carry in my bosom
Flowers and fruits enough for pleasure.
Withered!   Nay, your eyes deceive you.
Poison !   Why, your fancy's wild.
Go your ways, I'll rest and laugh—
Laugh at futile toil and grief.
It is my object to forget,
Since remembrance is but woe."

Stung with all this selfish speech,
He turned aside to seek relief,
But on every side was trouble.
Oft he wondered why such nothings
Still caused men to toil and fight,
And it passed across his mind,
" If but brothers would be brothers,
If men would be truly brothers,
Surely, with their loving labour,
Strong, united, healthful labour,
All this arid desert plain
Again would 'blossom like a rose.' "
Thus he thought to stem the strife ;
But his efforts proved in vain.
Buffets, scorn, contumely his,
Which he had no force to meet ;
Even seekers, pacing wildly,
Heard not, heeded not his words ;
And the sick, with fever wild,
Madly cast away the water

Which with peril he had brought.
Sickened with his useless toil,
Knowing not that to succeed
You must never shrink or tire,
Longing came for peace and shelter,
Rest and shade and flowing water,
Some relief from hideous warfare,
From the beastlike strife of men.

Through the mazes of a thicket,
Over arid dusty plains,
Through a thorny wilderness,
Stung by snakes in tangled coverts,
Pierced with thorns, fatigued, bewildered,
Yet he fled, and fled in vain ;
Till a toilsome steep ascent
Led him up a mountain height.
Spent and weary, always climbing,
Came he to where giant rocks
Stood to bar his onward course.
But he then perceivèd where
Those great rocks, like palace portals
Parting, showed where fresh and green
Moss and sward, with rose and myrtle,
Offered rest and shade and peace.
And amidst, uprising ever
Upward, upward to the sky,
With a never-ceasing music,
With a light and with a glory,

There a living column rose,
Shimmering in wondrous radiance,
Gleaming in eternal Day.

"Glorious fountain, have I found thee?
Living water, art thou here?"
Thus the pilgrim; but he saw,
Like those guarding fabled Eden,
Forms majestic, silent, awful,
By those portals sternly guarding
This new Eden from the world.
And within, a stately throng
All around the fountain standing.
Then, with sudden strength endued,
Lost all sense of weariness,
Lost all doubt and hesitation,
He is only strongly conscious
Of a new absorbing longing.
No more pining for the past,
For the dewy dawn of day,
For its freshness and its vigour.
This was all behind him cast,
As, with eager eyes, he spoke—
"Hear me, tell me, silent great ones,
By your beauty and your lustre,
By the calm that dwells around you,
By your still and silent strength,
Tell me, are you gods or men?
Hush, my soul, they will not answer,

Speak again, but do so wisely.
Mighty angels, pardon me,
But I pray you answer this,—
By my suffering mother Earth,
By the souls that thirst and pine,
By the souls that die in slumber,
By the many steeped in wrong,
By the souls that daring, striving—
Striving, working, ever onward,
Those who, weeping tears of blood,
Feeling dumbly, seeking blindly,
Find no hand outstretched to save,—
Tell me, must creation, groaning,
Live for ever in contention ? "

Silent are those curvèd lips,
Locked in ice those tranquil features ;
Yet he thought the eyelids, raising,
Thus a gleaming light displayed.
Was it scorn, or was it pity ?

Spake again the tired wanderer—
" I will tarry night and morning,
I will know no sleep nor rest,
Find no pleasure, no delight,
Till I read the riddle clear,
Which must solve the woe of man.
I conjure you, pray you, tell me,
Is there not some cure for this ?
Give me but this boon, I pray."

Then a wondrous music sounding—
Such a diapason sounding—
Almost fiercely broke the silence.
It filled the air, and shook the fountain ;
Then more softly, sweetly rounding,
Like harmonious voices blending.
And that fountain shimmering broke,
All its stately column fell,
Till it rose, it upward rose,
Higher, fairer than before ;
And in strange majestic movement
All these forms passed to and fro,
Weaving circles round the fountain,
In a rhythmic measure moving,
While they chaunted thus in chorus—
" We are spirits of the past,
We have also toiled and suffered ;
But life's riddle we have read."

Then that magic circle parting,
From amidst them there arose,
Gliding forth, a stately form.
Hers a strange and mystic mien ;
Eyes like ardent wells of fire,
Flooding forth a stream of light,
Shone as if aloft, afar,
From the lofty head, thrown back
On its snowy slender pillar,
As a distant gleaming Pharos

Crowning rocky pinnacles
Shines and smiles on surging seas,
Touching lightly angry waves,   ·
To the tempest-stricken sailor
Sends a ray to calm and save.

Then her lips, unlocking, parted;
But she stood as if enthralled
By some distant vision seen;
Those deep wells, her eyes, became
Cold and still.   The light was sleeping
On the tranquil depths below.
Then again arose a murmur
As of some bewitching music,
Stronger, clearer, still resounding,
Thrilling through the very being,
Magnetic, thrilling, almost pain,
" Smiting all the chords " of being.
Then a voice's harmony,
Thus enchaining, thus subduing :
" Mortal, wouldst thou know my life,
Know my life to learn thine own,
Quaff its bitter and its sweet,
Learn its wisdom to distil ?

" I was but a Roman maiden,
But the daughter of plebeians;
In my veins patrician blood
Never flowed and never mingled.

Wealth and lineage were not mine,
Cared I nought for name or fame,
Yet within my inner being
Longing sometimes strangely stirred :
Sometimes like a pure white flame
On a vestal altar burning,
A holy flame that burns aloft,
Thus that deep and solemn longing
Burned within my childish breast.
I would live apart and free—
Free from cares of self and passion,
I would live a life devoted
To the gods and public weal.
Then anon my brain ran fire,
And a fever seized my being :
I would be like other women ;
I would be adored, adoring ;
I would love with passion's fire,
One who loved me long and well—
His the great and noble spirit,
Mine the task to help and praise,
Mine to smooth his daily path,
Mine to be his all in all.
Then, again, in other mood,
Self-sufficing, self-subduing,
Said I, ' I will never seek,
Never wait for human love.
There are none so great and godlike,
Yet so manlike in their struggles,

Can command my loving homage,
Yet can need my tender care,—
None, none for whom I could subdue
All this soul within me rising.'
Yet there would a yearning seize me
To be kindly to my kind,
To be womanly and loving;
And when men bowed low before me,
In their slavish foolish passion,
Still a yearning sometimes seized me,
Yearning for their sickly sorrow,
Yearning to give love for love.
Why this wasted world of passion
Given to one who cannot use it,
Wasted at my stubborn feet?
Yet I turned in sudden loathing—
Turned and fled with scorn and dread.
Then I saw the Roman matrons—
All those stately Roman matrons,
With their noble sons and daughters.
All their duty was their pleasure,
All their pleasure was their duty.
Proudly reared they sons for fame,
And their daughters might become
Mothers of a race of gods.
Then, at times, a dark-eyed boy,
With his falcon eager face,
Would come listen to my tales,
As I sat hard by the portal

Of some palace or a temple,
And, in listening, he would say,
'Oh, if you were but my mother,
Thus to talk to me and teach,
I could fight like noble Hector,
Or, like our own Marcus Curtius,
Die to close a gulf of woe ! '
Or a girl, with brow of snow,
Serene and pure as mountain-top,
Would, in drooping her dark lashes,
Murmur, 'Oh, that I could die,
Die like lovely Iphigenia,
Die to save my countrymen ! '
Then, in one long close embrace,
Close to all my empty heart,
I have said, thus clasping fondly,
' Gods, if these were only mine ! '
Then I saw how rank and state
Were but other names for power,
And I knew how men misused them,
How they bartered wealth for pleasure,
How great names were sold for pelf,
How a nation's freedom often
Was but sold for place and power ;
But methought, ' Were I so gifted
With world's strength and wealth and state,
I would, like some bounteous river,
Flow in happiness and goodness,
Blessing, gladdening, as I went,

Driving winter from my shores,
Thus perpetual springtime making;
All amidst joy and rejoicing,   .
All should lead a festive life;
Far and near, and all surroundings,
Thus would prove a heaven on earth.'

"But a voice within me surging
Spoke in sorrow, spoke in pain—
' Maiden, you are not for pleasure;
Not your life is given for joy,
Not your beauty is for pleasing.'
Then I said, ' My youth burns in me :
Fain I would be like my kind,
Fain would I be loved and cherished,
Fain live, like the world, for joy.'
But that voice with clearness answered,
' Maiden, deep within your bosom
Is a glorious fount of wisdom;
Not for riches, not for splendour,
Not for glory, rank, or fame,
Must thou barter that within.
Maiden, pause to think and ponder—
Not for all the tenfold blessings
Of a life serenely gay,
Not for all the charm of living
Like a Ceres in thy plenty,
Giving as thou hast been given,
Must thou barter that within.'

Then I answered, 'But I feel
That a wealthy world of love
Is mine to give, most freely giving,
Asking little in return.
Does the sun that gives its rays
Ask for light and warmth again?'
But I heard that voice replying,
'See, that gift is thine already,
Thine a wealth untold to give ;
And, behold, the Great All-wise
Waits to see thou use it well.
Not for merely earthly love,
Love for beauty, love caressing,
Not for all its deep enthralling
Must thou barter this great gift ;
Love with thee all sanctified,
Love with thee all purified,
Free from every wild delusion, —
Such alone must be thine own.
See thou dost not sell thy birthright
For a merely earthly thrall.
Thine a gift for all mankind.'
Then I trembled and I shuddered,
Drew my veil, and wandered forth
Through the market and the forum,
Wandering sadly, seeking dumbly,
Seeking for I knew not what.
Saw the gods, and praised their beauty,
For the artist's hand had wrought

Finished forms of god-like stature,
And had named them all divine.
Soon I, loathing, turned away;
For I said, 'These gods have wronged me—
Sitting in their cold calm state,
They have willed me love and beauty,
Warmth and life, and throbbing pulses,
And they are my wrong and curse.
What are we poor men and women?
Almost perfect and divine—
Perfect, yet with weakness clogged;
Half of marble, half of clay;
God-like in our great desires,
Worm-like in our puny power.
Gods we are in mighty wills,
Insects in our fragile purpose.
Like gods! but gods in fetters bound,
We touch the earth and feel our chains;
Our very powers bewitch and mar us.
Marred and enslaved, we toil and grovel—
Grovel on this our weary earth,
With blinded eyes, enfeebled powers.
No gods, no gods, this wrong committed;
There must be some other reading,
Other solving of this riddle.'
Thus I almost cursed these gods.
Then to Heaven, in mine anguish,
Cried for light and truth and wisdom.

Long I called, and long I sought :
Sought for light, as dungeon slave
Yearns to see the light of day.
Only thus I found some peace—
Peace in firm resolve and duty ;
For again that voice would say,
' Wait, and do thy part, and fear not ;
Wait, in time the light shall break,
And thy lips be touched with fire.'

" I had but one parent living :
He, my father, ever striving
For some world beyond his own.
Did ambition rouse his manhood ?
Nay, when in the noisy forum,
Midst plebeians fiercely crowding,
He would speak in words of fire,
And with deep impassioned accents
Stir their souls, they knew not why ;
Yet unmoved and calm himself,
He would heed nor praise nor blame,
Never striving to be first ;
But to human common feelings
Ever seemed he cold and dead.
Yet he almost showed a pride
In his only one, his child ;
But he never spoke caressing
Words of gentle import, never.
Only once, in early days,

Stroking back my hair, he said,
'Tell me, child, what think'st thou, tell?'
When he sickened with a mortal
Sickness that no man could cure,
Then the torch that burned so fiercely
Seemed to flicker, fade, and wane,
Till the noble spirit, changing,
Veiled the clearness of his mind.
Now, then, many sought my beauty,
Sought again the lowly maiden.
From some, I only turned aside
In my silent detestation;
But to one who simply, nobly—
So I thought then—offered all,
All his life, his wealth, and state,
Fain I would have proffered thanks—
Warmest, fullest, kindest thanks;
But he added, 'See, he knows not
Even you, his own sweet daughter:
In my mansion there are slaves
Shall take all the trouble from you.'
Then the mantling colour fled
From my cheek, and left it cold,
As I turned away, and said,
'Here, beside my father's couch,
Here I stay to cheer his age.
Not to be the great man's wife,
Will I leave him to a slave.'

"But he died—my father died.
We were left alone together
In that last, life's lonely struggle.
No voice broke the solemn silence,
Save when once he murmured softly—
'The great Heaven bless my child.'
Then he roused, and pointing slowly
To the blank unpainted wall,
Said, 'See, thy words are there on fire;
Read them to me, ere I die.'
Then, sinking back, great silence fell.

"Thus we parted, thus he left me,
Thus alone, alone and free—
Oh, so young and sadly free!
And I said, 'Why thus forsaken—
I alone on earth, forsaken?'
But a voice said, 'Maiden, fear not.
Thou hast so far done thy part;
Listen to the voice within.'
Yes, I listened very calmly,
Sought for light and sought for wisdom,
Hardly knowing how to pray,
Little knowing all I asked.
Long I thus remained in stillness,
Till, one day, by a temple's wall,
I watched the crowds of people pass,
Saw the forum shadows lengthen,
Heard the hum of voices dying;

Then I rose up from the dust,
Went forth to the purple Campagne,
Saw the god of day retreating.
Floods of crimson and of gold
Lit the city and Campagna,
Lit the temple and the tomb.
But I said, ' There is no God ;
Glorious is our world in beauty,
But its Maker is unknown.'
Then I bowed my head in sorrow,
Bowing down in anguish, saying,
' Are we thus for ever striving, '
Seeking for we know not what ?
Then, uncared, unheard, descend we
To the grave of baffled hopes ?
Are those empty sculptured tombs,
Or those mouldering dusty urns,
All for which we live and learn ?
And those stars that, from above,
Seem to watch with radiant eyes
All our struggles and despair,
Yet unpitying eyes unmoved,
Are they all self-planted there ?
Are they truly gods and heroes
Who have lived their day on earth,
Yet for ever in their splendour
Smile upon our wretched world ?
Lived they here, committing crime,
Yet live they there in slothful ease,

Fanned by airs ambrosial, fragrant,
Fed on godlike food and nectar,
Pillowed on a roseleaf couch ?
Gods, I scorn such weak enjoyment !
Gods, I scorn your heaven and you.'
Full of anger and contention,
I then heard a distant muttering,
And I knew the tempest's moaning
As it swept the waste Campagna.
Soon aloud, in stormy accents,
Fiercely loud the tempest spoke.
To me it spoke of demon rages,
Like the angry voice of men
When injustice, rousing madness,
All their untamed passions rage,
Or, when in the vast arena,
Like the lion scenting blood,
Thus they rave at sight of prey—
That prey, their fellows and their kind,
Torn, tormented, mutilated.
Thus the lightning's vivid flashing
Seemed like angry eyes of men.
Yet I saw another likeness—
Saw how in myself was raging
Such a storm, untamed in fierceness,
Rifling all my life of sweetness,
Filling all my soul with gall.
Then I saw, and gazed and wondered,
For it was as strong reflection

Of my warring soul's desires,
Of my mind and spirit's striving,
Of my will, untamed and daring,
Of my spirit seeking wildly,
Of my reason, blind but strong.
Black as Styx was all Campagna,
Save where lightning tongues of fire,
Or its sweeping sheets of flame,
Lit the plain both far and near,
From our Rome to far Soracté.
In that light the wondrous desert,
Rich with verdure, flower-strewn,
Showed like ruin, wreck, and chaos,
In a gulf of livid flame.
I turned aside to seek a grotto
Where to hide my aching sight,
But, like one by spell enchanted,
There I gazed, and still I saw,
In that ruin and that chaos,
But a type of human discord,
Human passion's fatal discord
Working ruin, desolation.

"In the cave at last I rested,
In the ferns I hid my face,
Half asleep I murmured faintly,
' Is there God who tames the storm?'
And I slept till morning dawn.

" Fairer than my tongue can tell,
Fairer than the fairest dream,
Was that Campagne when I woke,
Still and calm as babe in slumber
That has cried and laughed to sleep,
With the tear-drops on its lashes,
And lips parted as in laughter.
Not a trace of storm or passion,
Only dewlike raindrops, quivering,
Hung upon the ferns and tree-knots,
Rested on the grass and moss.
Clear and calm the twilight blue,
Very clear the cloudless sky,
As I stood amidst the silence :
Watched the blushing of the dawn,
Saw Aurora gently rising
From her rosy eastern couch ;
Saw Apollo, god of day,
With his fleet and fiery steeds,
She pursued and he pursuing,
Till she vanished in his glory.
That great Day-god conquered all :
His radiance fired Soracté's height,
Crimsoning all its snowy brow ;
Then, descending in his might,
Turned streams and dews to vivid gems,
Diamonds shimmering, many hued,
On each blade and fern transfigured.

" Up rose joyous insect life ;
Life rose in myriad forms of life—
Life, lusty life ; earth teemed with life—
The sound, the song of happy birds,
The calls of many lowing herds—
I heard them all.   I felt anew
Life might be loving, noble life,
Without a thought of self's desire ;
A life all clear.   Such life of love
I knew, I felt, then rose to praise.
Did I know God—the God of Love ?
No god of greed, of fierce desire,
No god of weak and selfish longing,
No god who, with a man's revenge,
Wars with mankind with human spite,
Then, resting in voluptuous ease,
Forbids sad mortals to enjoy.

" One God—all goodness, power, and might,
Are One ; thus all of good and great,
All wisdom, light, and love are One,
All pure, all perfect, all divine.
From hence the hero who bestowed
Fire, warmth, and light to suffering man.
It seemed to me creation spread
A golden book who runs may read.
I saw its scroll, so fair and clear,
Yet marred by man's foul, feeble pen ;
In many a fable and a myth,

He lost the glory and the truth.
Oh, talk of evil ! Man alone
Creates all evil and his woe ;
Yet in his subtle art divine,
Art full of godlike beauty still.
We know the fallen hero race,
And dream that once men were as gods.

" In my home again, I waited,
Pondering on these wondrous truths,
Seeking long for light and wisdom.
Then, like words of fire they shone,
Words of fire upon my wall,
And I seized my pen and wrote.
At last I heard as if one spoke—
' Go, this wisdom is not thine ;
Give it, as thou hast been given.'
Deeply, painfully I struggled,
As I felt the warm blood curdle,
Then surge wildly at the thought,
That to all the strange and distant
I must give my inmost soul.
' God,' I cried, ' Great Goodness, spare me !
If I had but little children,
All my sons would I instruct,
Lead them forth with dauntless brows,
Till, like great and holy prophets,
They might teach the world anew.'

"Then again arose a thought,
Speaking to my very soul,
And it said, 'It is not your own—
Not your words and not your being,
That will thus unveil to all.'
' Not mine own that I unveil
To the idle gaze of men ?
For the lowliest of mankind
Goodness lives and works for ever—
Shall I hinder in that labour ?
Rather, give them all my best.
Come shame, come scorn, contemptuous pity,
I care not, let my words be known.'
Then I rose and wrapped my volumes
Carefully in Eastern silk,
And I chose some seemly garments,
Simple, stately, in their fashion.
As I paced the lofty halls
Of the palace of the Cæsars,
Loud and high my throbbing heart
Beat, but not with woman's fears,
For I felt as though a queen
Came to speak some potent will.
Yet I felt as though a servant
Humbly bore his master's wish ;
To the Cæsar felt as queen ;
Thought of suffering, wayward people,
And the goodness they defile ;
Then I felt as humble slave,

Bound to work a sovereign's will.
It would ill beseem me now
To tell all that passed within
Cæsar's audience chamber there,
Nor how often I have climbed
Up those lofty palace stairs.
Ready audience Cæsar gave,
Smiling, gracious, careless ever ;
But at last, I said, 'Oh, Cæsar,
In thus scorning these my volumes,
In thus carelessly rejecting
All the wisdom that I bear,
You have read your sentence right ;
You have read the doom of Rome !
Oh, Rome, my Rome, unblessèd city,
Where your children never worship
Pure, Divine, Almighty Goodness,
But bow down to men and devils ;
Where you clothe your grandest heroes
In the filthy bloodstained raiment
Of vile, sensual, weakly men ;
Where in gluttonous feasts you revel,
In brimming wine-bowls spill your souls.
Rome, thrice crowned with lustly pride ;
Rome, where Vice is rich and jewelled,
But Virtue is in sackcloth clothed ;
O Rome, my Rome, thy day grows darker,
The time draws nigh : this golden palace
Will be but a waste of weeds,.

And the forum and the temple
But a litter for the cattle !'

" Then, while Cæsar smiled in scorn,
I had passed from out his presence,
Never to return again ;
But I went and stood amidst
The noisy peoples in the forum.
All my fears were then forgotten,
As I felt a glowing fervour
And mine eyes seemed all alight
With a blaze of radiant glory.
I laid those volumes on a shaft
Of a broken column near,
Where a temple, yet unfinished,
Vainly sought to rear its crest.
Then I turned towards the east,
Spread those pages open wide,
Looked and saw the east aflame.

" Then a sudden deadly hush
Came on all that multitude ;
Such a silence, that my words
Sounded with a force I knew not,
As I spoke thus, calm and clear—
' People, you are living strangely ;
People, you are suffering sorely ;
For you live like beasts, not men.
People, you but worship madly,

Wicked men you call your gods.
Listen, men ; I ask this question—
Why religion and all art,
Why your orators and statesmen,
Philosophers, and priests, and poets,
You patricians, you plebeians,
From the forum to the temple,
From the palace to the hovel,
All are sinking, sinking slowly,
As a nation sinking, losing ?
I tell you, because men, not gods,
Feeble, selfish men, mere gluttons
Full of lust and vain desire,
Have invented weakly myths,
Filthy, foolish, crazy fables,
Births of vain and bestial passions.
They have made those gods and heroes
Who in heart ye must despise.
Yet, behold, how all around you
Seems the work of one Creator !
Jove ! Omnipotent Creator !
Part of all that is around us,
He in us, and we in Him,
Thus our bodies should be temples.
But so vilely do we keep them,
That they crush the soul within.
Yet how fair might be, and seemly,
Life as one, as one creation !
This great All, who is in all,

Is no man of vengeful passions—
Not a man with hungry longings,
Nor the hater of our kind,
Not the enchainer of Prometheus :
Rather, would he aid mankind.
He, Prometheus, he, the Titan,
Conqueror of every evil.
How I know this ?　Look around you :
All of good and wise and true ;
All of happy peaceful being,
All the men who love their brothers,
Who deny themselves the feeble
Pleasure-seeking of their fellows;
All who can arise superior
To their selfish wrongs and woes ;
All that rise, serene and calm,
Victors from the strife with evil ;
All the beauty that surrounds us,
There in nature, here in man ;—
All are pledges of great Love,
Types and pledges of a Love,
Love in goodness, Love eternal.
In the bad unruly being ;
In the fighting and contention,
In that strife for self alone,
Of the man who weakly yields—
To his senses still a prey ;
In his poor enfeebled offspring,
In all pestilence and famine,

You but see the wicked warring
Of the little with the Great,
Of the false against the True,
Of the evil with the Good.

" ' See, my friends, your sculptors, poets,
Have in marble and in fable,
Wrought forth images of gods ;
Yet at best they could but shadow
Types, reflections of the All,
But, by sense misled or blinded,
Often gave us falsehood's masks.
Listen ! Here, within these volumes,
You may wondrous truths discern.'
Then I took my precious scrolls,
And I held them up aloft.
' He who wishes may possess them.
They are plain and simple volumes,
Yet they hold your fate within ;
Clear, distinct to some, their meaning,
Others can no word discern,—
Mystic, or too foolish, seeming.'
I saw no hands outstretched to grasp
These, my scrolls, until mine eyes
Met the gaze of one who wrapt,
Wrapt in thought, stood quite apart,
Then I saw how he held forth,
Both his hands beseechingly.
Foreign was his garb and aspect,

Calm his outward air and mien,
Yet, methought, some eager passions
Lurked beneath, in iron thrall ;
But it seemed to me that wisdom
Lay behind that massive brow.
And I felt my pulses throbbing
As I spoke to one so great.
'Take these scrolls, oh, mighty stranger !
Only make men know them well.
Go, and good be with thee ever.'
Then I turned, and far I hastened.
How I left that crowd, I know not,
Only that a pathway opened,
And, while a great silence reigned,
Swiftly moving I passed on,
While, behind me, as I went,
All that pathway seemed to close,
Then arose a surging murmur,
Gathering like a rising flood.

" With a feverish longing seized,
Fled I to the wide Campagna.
There for nights, beneath the starlight,
Communed with the All in All.
What my after life became,
Stranger, little need be known.
All along life's weary furrows,
Had my seeds been doubtless thrown ;
And I know that, if unseen,

Still they lived to grow and be.
Perhaps my life in time became
Like some glad and glorious poem,
As they say a woman's should.
But, what is one life in the many,
What one poem in Life's Song?"

Then she raised her arm, and said,
" Come, freely quaff these healing waters,
Then go speak what thou hast heard.
Go, my brother ; not for thee,
Are these cool and kindly shades.
Can *one* rest while others wander,
Madly thirsting in the desert?
To that desert take thy life ;
Live it truly, till those wanderers
Learn to live in God-like love,
And man's desert is no more."

H

SOMETIME, tradition says, in the far ages of the long,
    long night,
Wise men in the East beheld a wondrous star, a star of
    might.
It led them far, it led them wide, but to no stately palace
    piled ;
It led them to a village inn, a stable, and a little child.
But why, then, did they meekly kneel, why lowly greet
    him as their King ?
And why those gifts of gold and frankincense before him
    freely fling ?
Enough that him they sought, they in their wisdom had
    unfailing found.
And now, what star's effulgent light, gleams on the far
    horizon's bound ?
Yet does this world of puny men see nought, say nought,
    they make no sound.
So blind or dull, harassed and hurried, choked like
    Crœsus with his gold,
They fail, for nought but dull care and pitiful pelf can
    they behold.

And yet that light! It comes, it glows, and a new era's
    day-star springs.
What long procession files along? The nations and their
    mighty kings—
Kings all uncrowned, yet crowned with thought; kings in
    all excellence that's wrought ;
Kings, kingly workers, by earthly power and earthly greed
    unsought.

Again it burns, it shines through the drear darkness of
    men's dullest night.
It rises, and it fills the vacant East with that great star of
    light.
They come, they come, those nations and their kings, the
    great, the pure, the wise,—
Come to that living light of love ; kings to that light which
    doth arise.

FAILURE.

WHAT is it that you greatly dread
That same drear day when flowers are dead,
And all life's fragrant blossoms shed,
And all its brilliancy has paled?
Some one will cry in scorn, " He failed,"
What failed to be as genius hailed?

Or is it rather that you fear
Your work has failed, and none read clear
That which has cost your mind so dear,
That which cost you strength and leisure,
The sacrifice of all free pleasure,
Given without stint or measure?

Nay, do not fear, be not afraid;
He whose object is his race to aid,
Who would not by applause be paid,
If but in earnest he would strive,
His work lives, is evermore alive,
In other minds must work and thrive.

He cannot fail. If only one
Has known his work, that work is done,
And its eternal life begun ;
If one eye only sees his art,
And, taking thus his work and part,
Has shrined it in his soul and heart.

It is passed on, a golden clue
To all that is of great and true,
The higher life—some dreaming view,
With dim hope, as if far away ;
It could not dwell with kindred clay—
Yet may be ours—even to-day.

THE DEAD LION.

Run to death, the hunted lion's down.
In at the death—the human hounds have won.
The anguished soul that fought the body's pain,
To raise, to help all men, not merely slain—
Torn limb from limb, with many a yelp and yell,
And fierce, derisive cries, " He made his life a hell.
See what it is to talk so tall of life ;
He could not keep a happy, healthy wife,
He needs must make her slave and let her toil,
While he lost health and heart in fruitless moil."

And she, poor soul, who gave up all for him,
Her kingdom-mind, her heart. her hope, though dim,
Yet, womanlike, must talk her sufferings over,
To the fond gossip who deemed a life in clover
Were better than to expend that little life
In fruitless efforts to abate his strife.

Go, little souls—if souls, indeed, you have, at most ;
Go, tear those gaping wounds, and loudly boast,

That all the world may see how great ones bleed,
And how they suffer while this is their meed.
Call men to see how petty thorns of life
Had jagged and torn them ere that final strife
Of death, which laid them low, and thus a prey
To eternal talkers to beguile their empty day ;
Or for soured failures thus to vent their spleen,
Men who would render even great ones mean.

But yours no blame, true-hearted, honest friend ;
Yours not the fault when, moved by duty to the dead,
To make men know the source from which they fed,
You trusted the enlightened, generous world,
And little dreamed of all the abuse thus freely hurled
At the Prophet before whom they once had kneeled.
So great their debt, you could not guess, that when
        revealed,
The man as man, all debt forgotten and annulled,
These swine would trample pearls they had not culled,
Content to abuse the wisdom yet unlearned
From the dead lion, now so bravely spurned.

Friend of the dead, you nobly did your part ;
Not yours the surgeon's knife that pierced the noble heart,
To prove why thus it throbbed, and why so fiercely beat,
Why sometimes cold, and yet anon at fever-heat.
Yours not the hand that probed his sufferings grim,
Nor yours to mark defects and carve the tender limb,
And bare her loving heart or slit the careless tongue.

To the brave critic, then, we owe these manly deeds,
As he flings to the Babel world the heart that bleeds.

O friend and master, was that life so much amiss,
Spent with grim force in one great toil to teach,
In one long effort man's many minds to reach?
His soul with mortal clay too sorely weighted;
Ever hasting to the goal, though oft belated.
Is it for this men hunt your memory down,
And gibbet you for scorn of fools, who feared your frown
In life?—Go, rabble, learn such work to do;
And if that toil must make you sadly rue,
Then learn at least to let the great rest in peace,
And leave to wolves to tear more lamblike fleece.
But, if in obedience to some long-loved friend,
One to stern tasks doth all his powers bend,
To give the world such gems, a noble prize,
Beseech you, do not teach that to be truly wise
He must masque his friend in some fair, false disguise.

THE SECRET OF HUMANITY.

SUGGESTED BY A PICTURE.

STRANGE face that haunts us evermore, like weird light
    on a troubled sea ;
In vain we try that light to veil, in vain we try that face
    to flee.
Through life its witcheries have wrought around men's
    lives a subtle spell,
Meeting in beaten ways of life, or in far lonely wooded
    dell ;
In mountain solitudes apart, or in the crowded haunts of
    men ;
In southern fragrant groves and glades, or midst some
    savage Highland glen ;
In the thick, reeking, crowded street, or by pleachèd,
    perfumed bower.
We meet it still, we know that smile, so old, so young,
    so fell in power ;
That haunting face I long to paint, just once I faintly
    would describe,

And thus perchance its spirit lay, that fatal power bind
    or bribe.

There, by the grey salt sea again, in what bewild'ring
    lurid light,

Amidst strewn wrecks and dire dismay.   Behind her see
    fast closing night.

What weight of years sits on that brow, and weighs those
    youthful eyelids white;

The curved lips part as if to speak, but only greet us
    with a smile.

A smile ! but what a smile is there, enough the strongest
    to beguile,

And yet we are fain to turn aside, and, shuddering, needs
    must quail,

As one who, passing a prison pile, would feel his heart
    to fail,

If told, "A secret this contains concerns your life and
    holds your fate ; "

Almost compelled to enter in, as he would pass the
    ominous gate,

Yet with a wrench he tries to turn, he shudders, falters,
    while he longs—

Aye, longs, yet loathes, as in some dream, when sorely
    tempted by strange wrongs ;

And yet why dread that lovely face, so wonderful, so
    sweet and sad ?

But now again it draws me nigh—such faces sometimes
    drive men mad.

E'en as I look, I seem to know that, in some far-off
    distant days,
That face, those eyes, had met me there, and troubled
    with entrancing gaze—
Eyes that reflect the sea, perchance, with its uncertain
    opal light;
Eyes which, half veiled by drooping lids, may tell us less
    of day than night ;
But eyes of all ages and all time, eyes that have ached
    with watching long
The ceaseless tramp of many men, and the tired nation's
    endless throng ;
Eyes that have longed and lured and led, then loathed
    their willing captive thrall ;
Eyes that have sickened at all waste of life, and watched
    its rise and fall.
Unfathomable grave grey eyes, now dark and drear as
    darkest night,
Now laughing with a laugh of scorn, filled with a cold
    and cruel light.

O secret of humanity, unlike the fabled sphinx of yore,
You ask no questions, yet how many thirst to learn your
    vexèd lore !
You greet us in life's many ways, and few would seek you
    needlessly,
Yet once men see your wondrous face, they cannot pass
    you heedlessly.

Seized with a strong desire, they yield them blindly to
  your fatal spell ;
Needs must they follow in pursuit, that ardent longing
  cannot quell.
Some wildly seeking you, pursue a phantom to the gates
  of death,
And forcing entrance there, they, dying, curse you with
  their latest breath.

ST. BRIAVAL'S BELLS.*

THE MAN'S STORY.

OVER the seas from far away
    My ship sailed on with birdlike speed,
And still methought I heard alway,
        St. Briaval's bells,
        St. Briaval's bells,
Swiftly my ship like any bird
    Sped onward, till the break of day
Threw rosy lights as I still heard,
        St. Briaval's bells,
        St. Briaval's bells.

But far away those bells ring high—
    'Tis cheating fancy hears their chime—
Far, far away she listens nigh
        St. Briaval's chime,
        St. Briaval's chime.

* Briaval is pronounced *Brevel*.

My sweetheart waits and bides my time,
   While hearkening there above the Wye,
      St. Briaval's chime,
      St. Briaval's chime.

At last with the tide I sped along
   Up the fair river, till above
I see St. Briaval's towers strong,
      Where loud bells chime,
      Where loud bells chime.
In the great hall I met my love,
   There in that hall where guests may throng,
She sits apart like some white dove,
      While loud bells clang,
      While loud bells clang.

I bid her meet me at the dawn,
   In the first blush of early light,
For well we knew her kinsmen's scorn,
      At Briaval's chime,
      At Briaval's chime.
St. Briaval's chiming in the bright
   Glad dawning o'er the growing corn
Of St. John's eve.   My own that night
      At curfew toll,
      At curfew toll.

She promised she would meet me there,
   Down in the valley where there chafe
The prisoned waters of Brockweir—
      At early chime,
      At early chime.

The angry waters foam and rave,
  But not a sign from my false fair,
And yet she seemed *so* fair and brave,
      At Briaval's chime,
      At Briaval's chime.

I gnawed my badge in angry shame,
  I hardly heard the waters roar,
My temples beat so loud. He came
      And gently spoke,
      I fiercely woke.
My boat was anchored to the shore ;
  I waited, still no sweetheart came ;
I waited. Then an oath I swore,
      By fair St. Briaval's
      Thousand devils.

In a maiden's whim was I thus cast
  Aside, like some worn glove or flower ;
For my mate whispered me, "She passed
      At Briaval's chime,
      At Briaval's chime,
With her young handsome kinsman Gower."
  Go nail my colours to the mast ;
By George ! no more in maiden's bower
      I hear that chime,
      St. Briaval's chime.

THE WOMAN'S STORY.

How strange it is that I sit here
Still listening to that clanging near
    Of full St. Briaval's chime ;
To think how gladly from my bower's
High casement in these lofty towers
    I waited for the time,
Which seemed so long and yet so brief.
The woods were in their greenest leaf,
    St. Briaval rang his chime,
For the dawning of that sweetest eve—
St. John's—when my love took his leave,
    But bid me wait a time,
And in one year he would return,
And claim me ere the fires could burn
    At St. John's festal time.
On St. John's Eve we would be wed,
What did he care if " Nay " was said,
    If I said " Yea " in time ?
Then as the festive day came round,
There was no happier maiden found
    Within sound of Briaval's chime ;
For I knew my gallant hero well,
I knew unless evil him befell
    He would prove true to time.

I wandered in the fresh green wood,
And filled my kerchief and my hood
    With fairy bells that chime,
Soundless but sweet, and roses pale,
And ladies smock, and bindweed frail,
    All flowers that twine and climb.
To dress the hall which he would grace
With his strong, manly form and face,
    While Briaval's bells would chime.
Maidens set glowworms in my hair,
They told me I was very fair—
    I listened for the chime.
They trimmed my hair till it was late;
But then—I went to meet my fate.
    "Up the steep way they climb,"
So I heard say; but I could feel
My heart thrum like my spinning-wheel,
    And loud rang Briaval's chime.
As I sat spinning in the hall,
Then, then I heard his dear footfall,
    His footfall's ringing rhyme.
What did I say?   What could I say
He said, " Put kith and kin away,
    Be mine for all long time."
I was an orphan, he my king,
My kith care more for gold I bring,
    They love the red gold's chime.
So when the morning came, I wore
The white gown he had praised before,
    In that bright summer time.

I

My cousin, who knew well my plight;
Fond brother, but no lovelorn wight,
    Sought me at early chime;
He "would not have me fear," he said;
" But if with Greville I must wed "—
    Now, hark! St. Briaval's chime—
He "knew that spies and foes were near; "
For him, he "held me far too dear
    To spoil life for all time."
So he " would lead me in the dawn,
By secret ways, like some shy fawn "—
    Hark! hark! St. Briaval's chime;
And thus we passed through woodland night
To cornfields lit with rosy light,
    While early bells did chime,
Till all those happy woodland ways
And tender cornfields seemed ablaze
    With sunshine for all time.
Then came my lover's trusty mate,
And said, "Our boat's aground—too late!"
    Do bells no longer chime?
" The spies are out, be secret then,
To-morrow's dawn at Hermit's glen,
    Before the bells can chime."
In vain that tryst I kept next day,
At St. John's early dawn alway;
    Oh, sweet bells, do not chime:
For he came not, and then Lord Gower,
" By all the saints," he said and swore,
    " I'll seek him to all time."

He sought, and sought, but sought in vain,
And I stayed lonely in my pain,
    Hard by St. Briaval's chime;
I look from my high lonely bower,
I look athwart the town and tower,
    Where Briaval's bells still chime;
I see where once my lover's ship
Sailed out in that faint far sea strip,
    And know that all, in time,
Somewhere, somehow, each faithful love
Will live again all time above,
    And bless St. Briaval's chime.

OUT OF ETERNITY.

OUT of Eternity? Surely it must be so;
How can we tell, how can we ascertain and know?
Out of the many ages of long distant Time,
Those weary stairs by which he ever has to climb,
Man comes and comes. With what an easy, careless air
Some, jocund, gladsome, mount Time's lengthening stair.
Anon they stumble, as they think to gain some height,
And, failing, fall. By heaven, a grievous sight.
What! all to climb again? And yet that stumbling soul—
Who knows?—may rise, and with new force himself enroll,
Revived in some fresh form, enrolled in some new corps,
Yet knowing not whence comes that strange intuitive lore.
Knowing, yet knowing not, wonderful soul of man!
That through this pitiless world must pass and pass again,
Seldom with clouds of glory, but torn robes soiled with
        dust.
Or sometimes trailing sadly fetters dimmed with rust;
Torn robes of ill-used time, or fetters of a crime.
And yet such souls may rise and climb, if slowly climb,

Gaining fresh strength and vigour, each step renewing life.
Those steps of many lives, of strong and earnest strife,
May cleanse the soul, renew the strength, reform the will,
Leading man on, a higher future to fulfil.
For who can tell but that such sick and weary soul
May yet be first to reach—though with long toil—the
     goal,
That happy goal, which yet is but the golden gate,
The gate of Wisdom, which may open soon or late,
Which leads man to eternal good, his only fate.
No place for hesitating fear, no need for weary search ;
It opens wide, it leads him on in his eternal march.

DEATH.

DEATH ! what a problem still thou art,
And yet of Nature what a part!
I hate thee, Death, with all my heart.

And yet I love thee, too, kind Death ;
I hate when thy strangling arms enwreath
Some loved one ; stifling life's free breath.

But when I think how those strong arms
Might fold some safe from all alarms,
And hide them far from foes and harms ;—

When I think of life's long weary lease,
Sweet Death, thou seem'st to bid it cease,
And whisper to the weary—Peace.

IF LQVE COULD REIGN.

I LEFT my greenwood home afar
To mingle in the strife and war
    Of full life's eager ways.
The warm, strong blood of manhood's prime
Pulsed in my veins like some glad wine,
    As in youth's earliest days.

What stayed my course, what barred my path?
I crushed each bar like sapless lath,
    Nor cared for gods or men.
I said, " I reck not rocks that cross
And dam my mid-life river's course ;
    They'll cross me not again."

Eternal youth, eternal joy—
This my fond fancy from a boy,
    As I still sported free.
And now again that glorious thought
To me new life and vigour brought,
    As spring's sap to a tree.

I moved afresh in Time's great march,
Paused not for doubt or new research,
 But heedless onward went.
Whither, I never asked or thought,
Nor what my careless vigour wrought,
 For good or evil bent.

Till in that swarm of fellow-men,
Which makes our world like some vast pen
 Of hungry beasts that feed.
(Aye, feed and breed and waste and die,
Befouling earth in which they lie,
 Like hot-bed sown with weed.)

Lost and confused, I, in my pride,
Would fight my way before I died
 To some great good and light.
Through thickets, and rough rocky ways,
I struggled to find greater days,
 And thus would upward fight,

Till, far above the clouds and storm,
I could not feel the sun's rays warm,
 Nor hear the bells that chimed.
For all earth's song was mute and still,
While I alone—I had my will,
 And upward ever climbed.

At first some friends, and even foes,
Came to encourage or oppose ;
 But they soon fell aside.

The nearest and the dearest stayed
Their steps, and, looking askance, said,
"He climbs too far and wide."

At last alone, quite, quite alone,
I stood on some high peak unknown,
So far from human ken.
Hemmed in by ice and snow I stood,
And then there grew a bitter mood,
Born of contempt for men.

I knew them all ; I seemed to spell
Their petty creeds and faiths too well,
Yet knew myself too late.
Why should I live in this dull scorn
Of all my kind ? Was I, then, born
For such a lonely fate ?—

To lose all tender human love,
To live apart so far above,
Amidst the ice and snow.
I, who had wrestled with my kind,
Now fain would have them of one mind,
Saved from contention's woe.

The very clouds forsook me here.
But in the dark I saw nought clear,
Save weakness, grief, and wrong.
As thus I thought, a little hand
Just circled mine with slender band—
How slender, but how strong !

Yet hardly heeding that slight touch,
Forsaken still I seemed as much,
  Nor heard a distant moan—
The moan of many suffering men,
As captives in some far-off den,
  With painful monotone.

Where I now stood, almost alone,
So high, so cold, I heard that tone,
  My ice no longer froze ;
For human love was standing near,
Divinely taught to guard and cheer,
  To understand all woes.

Then rose a light, so wide and clear,
It parted darkness far and near,
  That light of love divine.
And then I saw how widely spread
That light touched hovel, palace, shed,
  That light which might be mine.

It showed me how our human earth
Might yet awake to joy and mirth,
  And less of grief or pain.
It showed how sorrows, clouds and mist,
Might yet by sunshine's rays be kiss't,
  If great Love's light could reign.

TO MAZZINI.

PROPHET and warrior ! great soul of truth,
Your Christ-like spirit nobly filled its mission,
And yet men knew you not, for in good sooth
They showed more scorn and hate than admiration
For him whose great sin was the omission
Of all men's weakness.   Their poor, petty pride,
Their love of selfish glory, their ambition,
All these he scorned ; his work, his hope, world-wide,
Was liberty.   Could that sin find remission ?
Prophet of Freedom ! you would save your land,
Not from mere earthly tyranny, but the scourge
Of that more fatal slavery, that brand,
That stain, which from man's soul man cannot purge ;
That which destroys, who fails from self to emerge ;
That slavery to self destroys a nation.
It is numb to pain, and feels no passions surge.
Thus with the nation Mazzini fain would save,
Fain from such fatal sickness purge.

Mazzini, when at the last you saw your Rome,
The sun had set, Rome's day seemed truly done.
For you no hope, no friends, no land, no home ;
Through ranks of foes you passed ! Your glorious sun
Was set ? No, though no victory you had won.
Vanquished ? In a sterner battle you had led
To conquest, and thus a new career begun.
Your day was done, your sands were run, men said ;
But yours was a battle-field where never sets the sun.

World-wide your field, your enterprise, your light ;
Baptized in pain, by sacrificial labour taught,
You lived your life for man, and led him on to fight
Where base corruption seethed. And thus you fought
All tyrants, and the anarchy that wrought
Among high or low, like worms that house and breed.
Fought it, although, by pride and folly bought,
It masked as freedom, or boldly showed its greed.
And did men say that you had worked for nought ?

Peace ! He who loved Italy with love so deep,
Yet died a hundred deaths in this dull isle,
Now sleeps ? How tranquilly he seems to sleep,
By Arno, where his Italy's sun doth smile.
Does he then sleep, that great one free from guile ?
Nay, that man cannot sleep ; his noble soul
Lives on in other lives. We may not know awhile,
Yet shall we know at last. Few reach his goal,
But those who do pass on and thus beguile
Men to fresh conquest, new warriors to enrol.

He gave his powers, his very life, a gift.
And did he fail? That life so earnest and so grave !
Was it enough his fellows thus to uplift?
Fame was as nought, and nought the crowds that rave.
For wealth, power, fame, and name, he did not crave.
Can one ask more than this? the failure's rift
In that full "lute of love" was nought to one so brave.
In truth, God gave to him his greatest gift,
The Christ-like boon to live and die to save.

SONNET.

SOME say God loved him, gifts He surely gave ;
And yet men say, that those so loved by gods
Die young.   This was not his, though his to save
Great beauty from great wreck.   While madmen rave,
Angels wait calmly till such scorpion rods
Are snapped asunder ; and those men at odds
With all of good and beautiful and true,
Vanish while mighty ones their souls endue
With patience strong to work the work of gods.
Thus Michel Angelo, lingering here,
Seemed as if from a grander world returned.
As though he saw through time and felt no fear.
Nought were the shows of life to him who yearned
For the calm beauty of the Golden Year.

SONNET.

WHAT, then, must service still be scorned, decried,
Despised, miscalled? and yet, unless you enter in
That gate by which all greater lives begin,
That gate of willing service men deride,
To you, all real, all noblest life's denied.
You climb in vain, no higher post you win.
He who truly serves is fit to be a king ;
Who will not, on the threshold must abide.

True kings must ever serve early and late.
A willing service bears no touch of shame.
Whether you work or have to " stand and wait,"
Be willing servants though you gain no fame.
Know that in serving you have lived indeed. ·
Contented, then, have you not gained your meed ?

SONNET.

WHO was this man they called the good and great?
Did sycophants before him humbly bend?
Did he his smiles to careless folly lend?
And did he hold his court in purple state?
And did men cry, "He comes, Albert the Great"?
But did fools call *him* their glass of fashion?
Did he give loose to every passion,
Like that besotted king, once England's blight?
Nay, this man, though a stranger to this land,
Made himself but a servant of the nation;
Without declaiming loud oration,
Gave his great mind to every fresh demand.
And yet we only learned to know, too late,
The prince who taught us how to serve and wait.

SONNET.

AMERICA, strong child of British birth,
So beautiful, so strong withal, and great.
Who says you are not of our kindred earth,
Lies in his throat and well deserves his fate.
Scorning his kin, scorned in return by all,
Go, let him have his way and let him rot,
Safely secure beneath oblivion's pall.
America, thy name no man can blot
From off the roll of nations, till thy light
Has ceased to shine, a beacon on life's way.
But quenched in eternal, darksome night?
That cannot be, strong child of day.
All are our kin who bravely fight with ill.
Then, doubly ours, we join with heart and will.

WRECKS.

I HEAR the breakers on the shore,
On the long reef I hear them roar,
    And echo from that wall,
That lofty, rugged wall of rock,
As if those hungry waves to mock,
    An echo to appal.

The lights burn warm and bright within ;
But hark ! how loud and fierce the din
    Of that wild storm without.
Hark ! how it wails, this piteous wind,
As though in contest with its kind,
    It finds no peace throughout.

Throughout the wide world, does it seek,
A homeless wanderer, does it speak
    Of shipwreck, loss, and grief?
The firelight shines on panelled wall,
Fire fiercely burns with rise and fall,
    As if it sought relief

In a strong struggle with that wind,
Which none can "hold, or have, or bind,"
  For that fire is wreckwood.
It battled with the storms so long,
A noble ship resisting wrong—
  Wind's wrong and wilful mood.

How terrible and sad that wail !
It sweeps apast us on the gale ;
  While blue and green the flame
Of our wreck-fire, all through the night,
Shoots up afresh with eerie light.
  I marvel whence it came.
From what poor wreck ? But, hark ! a gun.
Fling books aside. The storm has won !
  The wreck-fire's burning low.
And far, though faint, the cry is heard—
Help ! help ! Let's hurry, give the word,
  And save wreck from the foe.

Out, out into the pitiless night,
That aids the storm to victims blight.
  Some wreck we cannot save ;
For in this stormy world of fight,
Many a wreck is the doomed plight
  Of men however brave.

Of men and women. Often fate
Brings cruel wreckage, and too late
  All help to fight the foe.

The foe, unsparing foe that brings
Despair that cracks the strong heart-strings,
    And drowns men in deep woe.

Upon the storm I seem to hear
The echoes answering far and near,
    Of life-long wreck and loss.
Oh, human voices, do you all
Vainly on human pity call?
    Then leave but wreck, remorse.

NIGHT COMETH.

" MEN, ye must work while it is called to-day."
So cried Wisdom in the green days of old.
But men are now no wiser grown, they say.
For centuries they heard those words of gold ;
And yet how carelessly they wandered by,
  Unmeaningly their lives those spendthrifts spent.
But now—to-day—we hear afresh this cry,
  Which, gathering force as if the air it rent,
Says, "Night cometh, cometh, when no man can work."
  Thus in men's ears it ever seems to ring—
"Night cometh." But do men know those shadows
    mirk,
  That like dotards to some childish play they cling?

How can men live in empty pleasure's pain ?
How satiated they are, how poor, yet palled,
While cries the world for help, as dry fields call for rain.
How like some beasts, too over-fed and stalled.

Little they know, who live as fatted carp in ponds,
   All the glad freshness of the living streams that flow
To meet the ocean.   Who lives in self's hard bonds
   Knows not the freedom of great Nature's law.

But, see, the shadows deepen, and we hear
   The rapid tread of many hurried feet.
Above all, a sound that chokes some hearts with fear—
   " Night cometh, cometh, Time's work is all too fleet."
Aye, ringing through the thick'ning dark, that sound,
   A voice that must be heard, repeating evermore
Words that goad and drive man like a beaten hound—
   "Night cometh, cometh."   Then a wail is heard
     around,
   " Shall never day arise?   No, never, nevermore ! "

How, nevermore !   But, though long past is day,
What strange light floods the some time-darkened sky?
And do men quail before that vivid ray?
Oh, tell us, Is this death or life?   But none reply.

SUNRISE.

Was it summer ?   Rather winter, with its stormy din,
Night, not day, while rain and hail bedabbled all like
    sin.
Full of flood and storm the once glad earth to me
    beseemed;
And yet was it so, or was it rather that I dreamed ?
I climbed a hill : through dull walls a gate stood open
    wide ;
And behold ! the earth and sea lay smiling side by side.
I dimly saw faint lights where the sun had sunk to west,
So all obscured, so storm-clouded, it seemed not like
    rest.
But afar in the east there was a strange golden glow,
In the sky, and on the sea, in one great pathway's flow ;
And ships were sailing sunwards, on forwards to the
    light,
While the unrest passed away of the long feverish night.
Was it sunset thus calming the weary world's strife ?
It was sunrise, fresh sunrise, the glad dawn of new life.

SUDDEN DEATH.

"From sudden death, good Lord, deliver."
Do we pray thus, and mildly shiver
Lest Death should clutch us e'er our prayer
Is spoken? What, then, do we not dare
Trust souls to Him who knows the time
When each has risen or ceased to climb?

If but mere cumberers, we must dread
Death, however calm and slow his tread.
And will this mend by our prevention,
Or some priest's tardy intervention?
If, indeed, we turn this world of ours
Into mere pleasant lazy bowers,
If earth we wilfully encumber,
On the sick-bed our souls still slumber;
But if loving Goodness, God, as friend,
In active love for man, our paths will wend,
Till, when at last we close our weary eyes,
On this fair world, we know that God is wise.

With happy trust we yield our prisoned breath,
And gladly meet release from healing death.

No longer beating wings against the bars,
With moth-like efforts to attain the stars;
Then failing, feebly grovelling on earth :
Rather prepare we for some higher birth.
Thus resting in eternal Good and Right,
We need not fear the fall of sudden night,
Trusting anon to wake in fullest light.

A WALL OF GLASS.

You wish to know our better selves ?
What ! ticket thought on labelled shelves ?
Words, paltry words, cannot express
Our moods, our thoughts, our earnestness ;
For all of these they're powerless.

Words sever like a wall of glass.
How clear ! and yet we cannot pass.
We think we see each other plain.
It's well, for truly it were pain
To know the strange disfigurement,
Thus wrought by that transfigurement.
We think we know each other's tone ;
But fickle laughter, feeble moan,
Across that wall is heard alone.

How false that vision is, alas !
Which we would touch behind the glass.
The hand seen through that crystal mass,
In loving friendship would we clasp ?
In vain ; that hand we cannot grasp ;

We only touch a feignèd hand,
Which often fails our hold like sand.
What truthful pressure comes athwart
That wall of glass so richly wrought?
What close familiar greeting thought?

The human pulse, electric dart,
Strikes coldly, far, how far apart;
Alone each dully bears his smart;
E'en from our dear ones the last sigh
Echoes but feebly, though so nigh.
Living, we could not understand;
Dying, in vain we would demand
Whither, oh, soul, to what far strand?
What cheered the night, how breaks the day?
What! does no answer light the way?

But Death! Death breaks the spell at last,
Shivers the glass, and frees the thrall.
No longer seeing darkly all,
Hands clasp, long parted by that wall;
Faces that far in severance frowned,
Disguised in hate, or sorrow drowned,
Friends dead to us, in anger bound,
Who yet in severance would repine,
Shine out; the same, yet new, divine,
If strangers once, now stand revealed.
All sorrows past, all wounds are healed,
No more we stand or fall alone;
We know, are known, and all are known.

FREEDOM.

BENEATH the sea they bid me gaze,
And there I saw, through golden haze––
Or was it but a beauteous vision,
Which mocked my careless indecision ?––
A city, with vast temples, towers,
A city of immortal bowers.
Immortal ! Nay, my vision lied ;
Drowned in oblivion's sea she died.

Dear Freedom, phantom, fairest city,
We seek and lose thee. Oh, the pity !
How long we sought, how poorly lost ;
At what great peril, what sad cost.
Lost, swamped beneath the treacherous sea—
That sea of Self. Lost Liberty,
Oh, nations, rouse you to attain,
Nor always seek, and seek in vain.
For wealth and power you ever fight ;
You make Right kneel to sordid Might.

Go, break your idols, lest they fall,
And crush the worshippers that call,
" These are your gods ; ye men, behold ! "
Gods ! Gods of clay, though smeared with gold.

TO THE NATIONS!—ANARCHY.

YE nations, tell us not of rights and wrongs.
Let men or peoples 'midst the mighty throngs
Living in this fast whirling, working world,
Let them raise their cry, with blood-red flag unfurled,
As is their wont, and howl, " Give us our right ! "
Such truly bear within a fatal blight,
Showing that slavery ever is their doom,
Fate that pursues them even to the tomb,
That tomb of baffled hopes, abortive schemes,
Fit end to childish struggles, empty dreams.
They shriek for freedom, but they shriek in vain ;
They know not law, nor can endure its pain ;
The law of liberty was never theirs,
Besotted as they are by lusts and cares.
Who cries to the world, " Help ! I am poor, oppressed !
Give me my rights, and have my wrongs redressed "—
Such men or nations nurse within the seed
Of sore disease, their powers waste and bleed.
These—truly victims of tyranny and hate—
Breed their own tyrants, and weakly yield to fate :
It is that perilous stuff that lurks within,
That death to which all weakness is akin.

In health men work by law, license they scorn :
All license is disease, of foul disorder born—
The coward, liar, the dastard, and the slayer,
The false, the assassin, and betrayer,
Trust me, such knaves, such blundering fools,
Or the rogues who are their dupes and tools,
Must be purged from out a healthy nation,
Or it sickens in plague's contamination ;
Aye, contamination, for its poisoned breath,
Fatal to all healthy life, works truly death :
This, their own sin and weakness, seals their doom,
And for repentance leaves but little room.
Thus among nations they will cease to exist,
Falling a prey to who may care or list.
Such is the fate of weakness and of crime
The fate of sinning nations all through time,
Anarchy's slaves they forfeit Law's fair princedom,
And so lose greatness, life, and all true freedom.

Beware, sad nation, if this is your case,
For then your day is done, you have lost your race ;
To some stronger State you must become the slave.
Night closes in, listen, and cease to rave.
Oh, weakling, the Cæsars that once scourgèd Rome
Could not work for you what folly works at home.
Be wise in time, quit you like men, be strong—
Strong in righteous law, the only cure for wrong ;
Strong in earnest thought, calm, patient labour,
Faith's sacrificial love, each for his neighbour.

SACRIFICE.

ON HEARING GLÜCK'S "IPHIGENIA."

HARK to that subtle music rare,
Clear notes that float upon the air,
That fall and rise, how sweet and fair ;
    But yet they speak of woe.
While mingles with them some far sound
Of winds forlorn that wander round,
Of shuddering waves, rock-fettered, bound—
    Those foaming waves below.

But hark, again, that louder swell,
Which seems all softness to repel
Triumphant notes !   I fain would spell
    The tale those sounds relate.
Yes, Iphigenia's grief I hear,
Music, wind, wave, voices clear,
Speak but of sacrifice and fear :
    Men grieve at such a fate.

You see her now, so young and slight,
Doomed by a savage will and might;
Well may she shrink from death's sad night
    And sacrificial knife.
Her light step could not crush the flowers,
With which thus crowned, her only dowers,
She simply waits to obey the powers,
    And save the Greeks from strife.

Inspiring music in your voice
I hear, and hearing can rejoice,
In strength of sacrificial loss,
    Which is but wider gain.
All through the world we see them fall,
Those martyrs to the good of all;
Why should their fate indeed appal,
    For do they die in vain ?

They die, "but make no sign," you say,
Cut off from each bright hopeful ray,
Which might have gladdened their poor day ; ·
    Aye, die without a sign.
A sign of what ?   God seals them there ;
Unknown to men, this signet rare ;
They meet their doom without despair,
    Nor think they to repine.

Unconscious martyrs, theirs no palm,
No crown is theirs ; they wait in calm,
Till some day they must join that psalm
    They never thought to sing:

L

That grand old pealing psalm of life—
Of life, of victory out of strife,
Of all our suffering world is rife,
     With which true song must ring.

Well might we envy those whose share
Of life, of work, to do and dare,
Yet leaves no space for carking care,
     No room for selfish thought.
Few know what rest, what perfect peace,
Is his who gives his life's full lease
For fellowmen, then finds release
     From all that earth has wrought.

Nay, grieve not when they say, " He died,"
One on whom living men relied,
Died in some cause too slight to abide,
     A sacrifice for nought.
Is ever sacrifice all lost?
We are such fools by passions tost,
And yet for ever counting cost,
     As if true life were bought.

Counting the cost! Oh, fool that cowers
For fear of loss, supine in bowers
Of ease, you lose your manhood's powers,
     And waste your golden seeds,
Your golden grain, on that hard shore,
Where hungry waves for ever roar,
Where waves of reckless pleasure pour :
     Go, reap its briny weeds.

MOTHER EARTH.

Oh, do not rail at Mother Earth,
   She is so sweet and fair;
She is a child of happy birth,
   And yet was born to care.
Perfect in form, of lovely hues,
   Not bred in sorrow's night;
Man came, and thus did interfuse
   Poor Earth with his foul blight.
In her kind lap I often lie,
   And then she seems to speak,
" Oh, child "—it is thus her breezes sigh—
   " Why, then, are mortals weak?

" Why with their bestial folly spoil
   My woods, my greenest glades,
My mountains even with their toil,
   Their moiling greedy raids?
Why with contentions will they dim,
   And render dark and cold,
All that my artist once did limn
   In hues of blue and gold,

With softer shades for sadder minds,
    And still for all the glow
Of kindly sun, with kindly winds,
    That do but gently blow ? "

Yet when by strange convulsions torn,
    Dear Earth, it seems to me,
You make man wish he were unborn,
    He knows not where to flee.
No safety on his mother's breast,
    No shelter anywhere,
For him there seems no place of rest,
    Thus rent by fear and care.
" Yes,"—thus the answer softly sighs,
    "The paltroon always fears ;
He talks so loud, all right defies,
    Nature he never hears.

" It needs my darkest, fiercest mood
    This paltry man to teach
That Nature is not understood
    By those who rant and preach
Their own crude thought and fond conceit.
    But those who serve yet wait,
Who do not spend their all for meat,
    With courage to be great,
For such I spread my fragrant flowers,
    And yet when storms arise
These will not shrink as he that cowers
    At every stern surprise."

ALONE.

A LETTER TO A FRIEND.

I.

Is it your fate, my friend, to stand alone,
Apart, perforce, from most men's little creeds?
And yet some ask, " For this what can atone—
To be alone, with such a wound that bleeds,
     And faint at evil deeds?"
Some shrink, and faltering say, " I *am* alone,"
When fears thicken, as they will with almost all.
Perchance they mutter prayers and weakly groan,
Yet have no trust : their God does but appal ;
     For help they wildly call.
To such, nature is but chaotic horror,
Swayed only by strange fits of Demon hate ;
And God, amidst confusion, wrath, and terror,
Seems distant far ; while they are lost in error.
Their God, then, is a thing of fate?
On Him, at least, they do not wait.
Truly, at times, strong forces seem arrayed,
Stamping Truth and Beauty into formless dust
     With cries of Will and Must.
Such savage forces with all evil mate,
Vile armies with vile banners well displayed
Fill hearts with grief, making men sore afraid.

II.

This is not yours, my friend,
Not yours to weakly bend,
In that you trust in that strong goodness all Divine.
What if this sky is dull and sear ;
You know, when cleansed from doubt and fear,
It is great Heaven's eternal dome, both yours and mine,
Where light and love and truth for ever rest ;
No terror can long dim that perfect light of Love.
    This earth, some deem so sad,
Glows when that ray has touched its weary breast,
And in its thousand hues reflects all heaven above.
    Are we, indeed, so mad
    That we ourselves must lend,
    Lend to all darkness drear,
    Boasting that Evil's best,
    Seeking in vain for rest ?
Oh lift us from Earth's mists ! let us be glad,
Glad in that light which, ever like a dove,
Broods over all, till even chaotic wrong
Is tamed, subdued, where ever love is strong !
Ay, glad in that love, your faith can bear the test ;
For you the sun still shines behind the darkest cloud ;
    Beneath the mantled snow
    Earth's fruits still live and grow,
And flowers are budding yet below their shroud.
From you no power this happy truth can wrest,
The truth which bids you trust your God, and know
You are alone with Him, and thus need fear no foe.

FAREWELL.

I ASK these verses, will they ever meet the eyes
Of friends belovèd ? will such learn to prize
My earnest speech ? will it aid some other lives,
Treasured, mayhap, as honey stored in hives
For use in wintry sadness, and thus my rhymes
Become as household words, when in future times,
My dead self lives again, useful, understood,
As it could not be 'neath life's disguising hood ?

To some the light has shone through many prisoned life,
Through all its stifling cares and heavy clouds of strife ;
And yet how hard it is to speak out all they know
To those who sit in darkness, and cannot see the glow.
Thus as we pass long vistas closed by fading day,
We hear some bird in twilight troll his parting lay,
Singing, not waning glories, but joys of coming dawn.
The crowds go by, and if they hear, it is with passing
   scorn.

Some sick with toil or care, and some with honeyed
    pleasure,
But few who pause to hear that bird's high farewell
    measure.

Can I, then, dare appeal to just one careless ear?
If only one could know, if only one could hear,
Truly if some light has come through life's many prisms,
Through all its choking cares, its toil and endless schisms,
I cannot but desire, from out my poor endeavour
Some finer spirit yet may draw a fairer treasure,
As finds skilled workman in the quarry's marble floor,
The future statue lurking, safely hid in store;
Known by the practised eye, carved in more skilful wise,
Revealed to gladden and delight even saddest eyes.
And thus from my frail song some thoughts may rise and
    shine,
Transmuted by fresh skill to "issues more divine."

THE END.

PRINTED BY WILLIAM CLOWES AND SONS, LIMITED,
LONDON AND BECCLES.

www.ingramcontent.com/pod-product-compliance
Lightning Source LLC
Chambersburg PA
CBHW021108020726
47500CB00003B/661

* 9 7 8 3 7 4 4 7 6 8 0 5 4 *